BLACKSTONE RANGER SCROOGE

Blackstone Rangers Book 6

ALICIA MONTGOMERY

Also by Alicia Montgomery

THE TRUE MATES SERIES

Fated Mates

Blood Moon

Romancing the Alpha

Witch's Mate

Taming the Beast

Tempted by the Wolf

THE LONE WOLF DEFENDERS SERIES

Killian's Secret

Loving Quinn

All for Connor

THE TRUE MATES STANDALONE NOVELS

Holly Jolly Lycan Christmas

A Mate for Jackson: Bad Alpha Dads

TRUE MATES GENERATIONS

A Twist of Fate

Claiming the Alpha

Alpha Ascending

A Witch in Time

Highland Wolf

Daughter of the Dragon

Shadow Wolf

A Touch of Magic

Heart of the Wolf

THE BLACKSTONE MOUNTAIN SERIES

The Blackstone Dragon Heir

The Blackstone Bad Dragon

The Blackstone Bear

The Blackstone Wolf

The Blackstone Lion

The Blackstone She-Wolf

The Blackstone She-Bear

The Blackstone She-Dragon

BLACKSTONE RANGERS SERIES

Blackstone Ranger Chief

Blackstone Ranger Charmer

Blackstone Ranger Hero

Blackstone Ranger Rogue

Blackstone Ranger Guardian

Blackstone Ranger Scrooge

COPYRIGHT © 2020 ALICIA MONTGOMERY
WWW.ALICIAMONTGOMERYAUTHOR.COM
FIRST ELECTRONIC PUBLICATION DECEMBER 2020

EDITED BY LAVERNE CLARK
COVER BY JACQUELINE SWEET
120220PM

Chapter 1

"**M**otherfucking ball sack!" J.D. McNamara cursed as a big glob of oil hit her on the cheek. Of course, oil, dirt, and grime were all part of being a mechanic and working with cars. But still, it was annoying as fuck.

Her inner animal didn't like it either. The feline sniffed at her distastefully, whipping its short tail around.

Damn prissy little thing.

Her inner feline yowled in protest.

Oh, J.D. knew her animal was fierce. It was dubbed as the deadliest cat in the world after all. But its small stature didn't exactly do them any favors, especially when compared to the other shifters in town.

While the population of Blackstone, Colorado, was made up of a variety of shifter animals, most were inevitably predators like bears, large cats, and wolves. However, she was none of those. In fact, she was a very rare shifter—an African black-footed cat, one of the smallest wildcats in the world. Few people knew who she was because ... well, it was hard to explain exactly, and inevitably, people would think she was just a cat.

"You all right there, J.D.?" came a familiar voice from above.

Finishing up the repair, she slid out from under the Toyota she'd been working on and looked up at Gabriel Russel's grinning face. "Yeah, yeah," she sighed.

"You didn't sound like you were all right," he teased, but offered her a hand.

She took it and allowed him to pull her up. "Yeah, well next time, why don't you get a money shot on the fucking face, Russel, and see if you like it."

"I'd tell you to act like a lady, but you'd probably knee me in the balls," he chuckled.

"Damn right." She grabbed a rag and wiped the oil from her face. "Besides, people who cuss are smart as fuck. It's a scientific fact." She threw the dirty rag at him playfully, but he blocked it with a hand.

"Whoa, watch the hair!" He shook his head, making his long, dark golden locks shimmer. It was almost comical and very apt—Gabriel was a lion shifter, after all, and was as proud of his human mane as he was of his animal's. "Just because you don't care about what you look like, doesn't mean some of us don't."

"Some meaning *you*." Taking her trucker cap off the hook from the wall, she placed it on top of her head. It was the only way she could cover her mop of unruly blonde curls. If she spent time on trying to tame it every morning to have it perfect the way Gabriel did, she'd have to wake up at five every day. "So, to what do I owe this pleasure, Russel?" Not that Gabriel needed an occasion to show up at her garage. They had been best friends since grade school after all.

"Oh yeah." He held up his hand, lifting up a white box. "Temperance wanted you to have this. Ginger pumpkin streusel pie. Her first Thanksgiving creation."

"Ooh!" Taking the box from him, she took in a sniff. The smell of ginger, pumpkin, and spices tickled her nose. "I'm honored, but what's it for?"

"For not charging her for the tune-up and oil change."

"Of course. You know what Pop always said. Family—"

"Don't pay," Gabriel finished with a fond smile on his face. "It means a lot to me. That you consider her family too."

"Like I wouldn't. She's your mate and soon-to-be wife, so of course she's family. Besides, anyone who can put up with you deserves more than free service," she said with a chuckle.

"Oh, ha ha, funny, McNamara, you should go on tour." Gabriel rolled his eyes. "Anyway, there's another reason I came here. Damon asked me to invite you to the Blackstone Ranger Thanksgiving party tomorrow."

"He did?" J.D. blinked. Damon was their other best friend, who was also chief of the Blackstone Rangers. Gabriel had been a ranger himself the past five years, but recently he'd quit so he could go into business with his mate to take over the local pie shop, Rosie's Bakery and Cafe. "I've never been asked before. I thought it was an event for rangers and their families?"

"Yeah, well, you're family, J.D.," Gabriel declared with a warm smile.

She stared at him, stunned, her throat closing up at the declaration.

Gabriel and Damon had been her best friends since she

was ten years old, when she and her father had moved to Blackstone from Brooklyn. She'd been the new girl in town, which already made her a target for bullies, and the fact that she was a tomboy didn't make it easier. But the two had stuck by her and protected her from mean girls who made fun of her for being a grease monkey's daughter. Yes, the three of them had always been tight, and they'd been with her through thick and thin, but, well ... none of them were the sentimental type.

"J.D.?" Gabriel asked, the corner of his mouth turning up. "Are you crying?"

"Fuck no. It's all the dust in here." She turned around and sniffed. "Don't ya have to be somewhere else? Like counting the gold bars in your trust fund or something."

Gabriel laughed. "All right, all right. So, I'll see you tomorrow? We're all helping out Dutchy with the decorations, and Temperance is bringing the desserts, so we'll be there early. Feel free to show up anytime, but we eat at five."

"Sure." She turned her head and flashed him a smile. "See you tomorrow. Tell Temperance I said thank you for the pie."

"Will do." The lion shifter waved goodbye and strolled out of the garage.

After cleaning up her tools and calling one of her mechanics to move the Toyota, she headed out to the trailer–office in the main garage lot.

"Hey, Pop," she greeted the photo that hung up behind the desk inside the office. Jimmy McNamara smiled down at her as he always did, frozen in time. He'd been too young when he died in that accident; barely fifty. Shifters couldn't get most illnesses, and they healed fast, but the truck that struck him down as he was crossing the street killed him on impact. His death had been a shock, and even now, a decade later, she still felt his loss keenly.

Even though she had taken over the business, this office was like a shrine to him—pictures of her as a kid and her mother, old school road signs, a black-and-white photo of the Brooklyn bridge, a classic James Dean on a motorcycle photo, and a framed and signed Billy Joel poster hung on the walls.

Sitting down behind the desk, she went to work checking her emails, inventory, and her accounting software. Finally, after what seemed like hours she was done, and she closed the laptop with a satisfying *click*.

"Whew!" Stretching her arms over her head, she leaned back on the worn leather office chair. This was not her favorite part of owning J.D.'s Garage, but it had to be done. "Yikes!" She winced as she saw it was already dark outside. It was the Monday before Thanksgiving, so they were busy trying to get all the repairs done before the holidays. *But at least I'll have the long weekend to look forward to.* Grabbing her jacket from the back of the chair and the keys to her truck, she headed out the door.

"Hey, J.D."

The unfortunately familiar voice made her freeze before she managed to finish locking the door to the office. With a deep breath, she turned around. "Hey, Roy," she greeted back, pasting a smile on her face. "It's pretty late. What are you doing here?"

Roy Jorrell grinned at her sheepishly. "Well ... I'm having trouble with my car."

She crossed her arms over her chest. "Again?"

He nodded. "Yeah. There's this *clunk, clunk, clunk* sound whenever I start it up."

"It's late, and I should be getting home. Maybe you can come back after the holidays?"

"But what if there's something wrong and I get stuck at home? Or on the side of the road?" He flashed her a boyish smile, his blue eyes twinkling. "Please, J.D.? You're the best mechanic in town."

Pop always said that you should never turn away business and to always treat customers well, but Roy was trying her patience. It was the third time this month he'd been in for some phantom sound or strange malfunction in his jacked-up GMC Sierra, but whenever she or one of her guys looked into it, his truck turned out to be perfectly fine. Why he kept coming back, she didn't know.

"Oh, all right," she said, resigned. "Let's go take a look."

She followed him to where he'd parked just outside the garage. "Go and start the car, and I'll check under the hood," she instructed him.

Minutes later, it was just as she thought—his truck was perfectly fine. "Nothing's wrong here," she said to him as she shut the hood.

"Oh?" He was suddenly behind her, startling even her own cat-like reflexes. "I could have sworn I heard something," he said, rubbing the back of his head with his palm.

"Uh-huh."

"So, you got plans for the holidays?"

"Yeah, I do."

"I'll probably just be alone," he said. "I didn't want to make the trip back to my folks in Florida since I was planning to see them for Christmas."

"Uh-huh," she said, trying to feign interest. "Well, I should—"

"I was wondering if you wanted to have dinner with me."

"Excuse me?" She stared at him, hands on her hips.

Roy had been a classmate back in high school, but he moved away junior year. He was some kind of avian shifter, if she recalled; he was mostly a loner at school, an emo kid who dressed in all black. But, like most people, he grew out of that phase and was some kind of computer programmer or something who worked from home. She ran into him at the diner last month, as he had recently moved back into town. That was when he started coming into the garage. *Is that why he'd been wasting her time?* Irritation grew in her, and her cat hissed, not liking this male one bit.

He swallowed. "I ... uh ... I mean, just to thank you. For being so patient with me."

J.D. thought about it for a moment. Roy was cute, she supposed, and he had a job and a full head of hair. What else did she want in a guy? She'd been dating actively for almost twelve years now, and he was a catch compared to all the losers she'd been with.

"J.D.?" Roy asked. "So? What do you think?"

"I think ... I think it's getting late." She sidestepped him.

"But what about that dinner?"

"I'll think about it, okay?" With a wave of her hand, she scampered to her truck. Shutting the door, she waited, watching Roy's truck as it drove away, then breathed a sigh of relief.

Why didn't I just say yes? She leaned her forehead against the steering wheel. Maybe it was turning thirty or seeing her best friends with their mates, but she was starting to get picky about who she went out with. Her last date had been months ago with an accountant she met on a dating app, and it had been *meh*. And the last guy she had the serious hots for? Well, he didn't even give her a second look. Besides, she was happy with her work, her life, and her social circle.

But now, all her friends had mates, including her last female friend, Dutchy Forrester, and she was starting to feel left out.

Sticking the key in the ignition, she started the car. Was she that oblivious that she missed the signs that he'd been coming to the garage to see her? That was it, right?

Maybe I should give Roy a chance.

Her cat hissed again.

"Oh, all right." Putting the truck into gear, she left the parking lot and headed home.

By the next day, J.D. had forgotten about the Roy thing and feeling sorry for herself for being alone. There were worse things than not having a boyfriend after all.

Besides there was no reason to be glum—not these days anyways. The holidays were her favorite time of the year. She remembered how magical it had been growing up. The cool weather, the food, the infectious cheer. Who could be sad during Christmas, for crying out loud?

The days leading up to Christmas always sent her into a holiday high, and she was pretty stoked for tonight's party. In the past, she and Pop celebrated Thanksgiving with Damon and his parents. Gabriel usually had to attend some kind of family dinner at the Russel estate, but he always managed to sneak off before dessert and join them. It was a tradition they continued, even after Pop passed and Damon was deployed and came back after being discharged. His parents had retired to Florida a couple of years back, but the three of them still got together on Thanksgiving. None of them could cook, unfortunately, so they would order Chinese takeout and watch football before her *favorite* tradition of all later that night.

Of course, this year was going to be a little different with the addition of two more people—Damon's mate Anna Victoria, and Temperance—but her best friends had assured her nothing would change.

And while she'd never been invited to the Blackstone Rangers Thanksgiving party before, she'd heard some stories about how amazing the spread was—turkey, mashed potatoes, sweet potatoes, cranberry sauce, green beans, corn, dinner rolls. *Mmmm.* Her mouth was watering just thinking about it. This morning, she made sure to put on her best Thanksgiving sweater—the one with a roasted turkey on the front that proclaimed "I like Big Breasts and I Cannot Lie." It was a big hit with the guys at the garage, so she was sure everyone at the party would love it.

After clocking out early for the day, she said goodbye to the crew and hopped into her truck. Since the rangers were in charge of keeping the mountains safe, their headquarters were located up in the Blackstone Mountains.

With the change in seasons, the trees and mountains presented a gorgeous view, making the drive a pleasant one, so she took her time. Eventually, she pulled up to the huge stone and log building, which stood at the entrance to the public area of the mountains, and parked her truck in the nearest empty spot. The party was probably going to be in the big cafeteria in the back, so she circled around the main building and walked into the open-air hall. Sure enough, the place was fully dressed to the nines in fall colors and decorations. She walked over to where Damon, Anna Victoria, Gabriel, Temperance, Dutchy, and Krieger sat down at one of the tables, which overflowed with wreathes, pine cones, ribbons, and other fall-themed accoutrements.

"It looks like Thanksgiving came in here and threw up all over the place!" she exclaimed, her eyes taking in all the fall harvest decorations. "I *love* it! Thanks for inviting me."

Damon rolled his eyes when his saw her sweater. "J.D. loves the holidays, in case none of you noticed."

"I do!" Seeing the empty spot next to Dutchy Forrester, she plopped down beside the fox shifter. "I mean, I love Halloween because that means it's almost time for Thanksgiving, and I love Thanksgiving because it means soon it'll be my favorite holiday of all time—Christmas! Woot!" She pumped her fist in the air.

"Oh God," Gabriel slapped a hand on his forehead. "I forgot what a nightmare you are during the holidays."

"I am *not* a nightmare," she denied.

Damon raised a brow. "Remember that time you dragged us to Verona Mills so you could see Santa Claus and then got us kicked out of the mall because you fought with Santa's elf?"

Oh yeah. How could she forget? As far as she knew, she was still banned from entering Verona Fair Mall. "That wasn't my fault," J.D. said. "He clearly lacked the Christmas spirit and needed to do a better job of representing the good elves of the North Pole."

"You called him out because he wouldn't let you sit on Santa's lap," Gabriel said.

"See?" She spread her arms wide, as if that proved her point. "Lack of Christmas spirit."

"You were sixteen," Damon pointed out.

J.D. harrumphed. "Unlike the sign they posted outside the Christmas village, the lyrics of that famous song didn't say 'to kids from ONLY one to twelve' now did it?" She stuck her tongue out at Damon and Gabriel, then turned to Dutchy, grabbing one of the rolls of ribbons on the table. "Can I help?"

"Sure," Dutchy said. "Here ... let me show you."

Her friend patiently showed her how to tie the shiny gold and orange ribbon into bows. *Hmmm, simple enough*, she thought. However, there was something missing with the wreaths. They didn't look festive enough. So, she decided to unroll the entire spool so she could make bigger and better ribbons. Glancing around, she found a bunch of what looked like leftover decor stuff under the table.

Oooh! She grabbed a handful of maple leaves, some pine cones, an ear of corn, and a mini pumpkin. It took a lot of work, not to mention cuts on her fingers, but she somehow managed to get everything on an empty wreath.

"Uh, so did I do it right?" she asked Dutchy sheepishly as she held up her creation.

"J.D.!" Dutchy exclaimed. "What did you—how did you even manage to get these maple leaves wrapped up in here?"

"What?" J.D. asked innocently. "I thought it looked festive."

"Er, it's certainly ... interesting," Dutchy said. "But ... let me give you some tips ..."

As Dutchy helped her put her wreath to rights, more people joined them, including Daniel Rogers, his mate Sarah, and her adopted brother Adam. Of course, where they went, Darcey Wednesday, Sarah's sister came, too, along with her mate, Anders Stevens.

"... but, great job, Dutchy," Anders said. When his gaze landed on J.D.'s wreath, he grimaced. "Now *that* looks like your handiwork, McNamara."

"Go fuck a French horn, Stevens," she hissed.

"Be a nice kitty now," he chortled. "So ... how about caracal?"

J.D. crossed her arms over her chest. "Nuh-uh, you're not going to make me say it." The tiger shifter had been impossible ever since he found out she had shifted in front of other people and was now trying to guess what she was. Well, he would never find out, not if she could help it.

Darcey rolled her eyes. "I apologize for my mate. I swear, I can't take him anywhere."

"It's all right, Darcey. Don't apologize for him." Getting to her feet, she turned to Anders. "However, I think *you* owe an apology to a tree somewhere for providing you oxygen."

"Hey!" Anders protested.

J.D. chuckled. "All right, I'm gonna go look for some snacks." She had forgotten to eat lunch since she was rushing to get all her work done, and now her stomach was gurgling with hunger. "I'll see you guys around."

Getting up from the table, she made her way into the main building. There was a vending machine somewhere on the first floor, but she couldn't quite remember where.

Since everyone was probably outside waiting for the festivities to begin, it was empty inside and half the lights had been turned off. She walked down the main corridor, tapping her finger on her chin. *Maybe it was by the locker room. Or the observation deck downstairs? Or—wait.* An idea popped into her head.

Damon loved peanut butter cups, and when she had lunch with Anna Victoria the other day, she had seen her with a big bag of them. When she asked who they were for, Anna Victoria said it was for Damon to keep in his desk so he would stop being such a grumpy bear when he was busy and forgot to eat lunch.

Heading down the darkened hallway, she made her way to the very end where the door to Damon's office was. She crept inside and dashed to the large oak desk, opening the bottom drawer on the right.

"Damon, you magnificent predictable bastard," she exclaimed when she saw the drawer overflowing with not only peanut butter cups, but also other candy. "Don't mind if I do," she cackled, ripping a packet of peanut butter cups and devouring both. Before closing the drawer, she stuffed her jeans pockets with more candy and chocolate. Satisfied with her haul, she zipped toward the door. As she prepared to shove her weight against it, however, the door swung open, and J.D. found herself sailing forward.

"Shit!" Momentum kept her flying until she collided with something solid and hard. "What the—*oomph!*" She landed on the floor with a hard thud, the wind knocked out of her. It took her a second before realizing that it wasn't the floor she'd landed on. No, she was right on top of someone. A living, breathing someone, based on the rise and fall of the chest she was now plastered to. "I'm so—oohhh!" A delicious male scent teased her nostrils, and she pressed her nose against the khaki fabric underneath her, taking a big whiff. *Hmmm.* That scent made her want to curl into a ball and wrap it around herself. Strangely, her cat felt the exact same way. *Huh.* Her prickly little feline *never* had an opinion on any male ... ever.

"If you wouldn't mind ..."

The smooth voice sent tingles across her skin. "Actually, I do mind—hey!"

She found herself being pushed away, then hauled up to her feet as warm hands gripped her arms. "What do you think you're doing, tossing me around like a sack of—" A gasp left her mouth as her gaze collided with the most unusual blue-violet eyes she'd ever seen. Even behind the gold-rimmed glasses, she could feel them examining her with cold, detached curiosity.

Mine, her cat purred from out of nowhere.

And his animal let out a triumphant roar as it answered back: *Mine!*

"Well, fuck me sideways," J.D. breathed out. "You're—"

"My mate," he finished, that cool stare never leaving hers.

The low, edgy growl that rumbled from his chest sent heat straight to her nether regions. "Oooh," she moaned, her knees weakening. *Control yourself, woman,* she chided herself as she leaned back to steady herself on the door. *You too, you little hussy,* she told her cat, which was now lying down on the ground, rolling on its back and showing its belly. *Oh, come on now. Play it cool.* That was the plan anyway, at least, until she lifted her head to meet those eyes again.

The icy, unaffected gaze slowly melted as his blue-violet eyes ignited with desire. Before she knew it, he pushed her against the door, his hands moving from her shoulders up to her neck and jaw as he lowered his head to hers.

Holy fucking moly.

His mouth attacked hers hungrily, like he'd been starving for weeks. Another growl sent her hormones through the roof. When she tried to move her hands up, he gripped her wrists and pinned them over her head.

Jesus Henry Christ, her panties practically flooded at the dominant move, and she melted against him. His lips never left hers as he continued to devour her, their kisses rough and wild as their teeth and tongues clashed. At some point he had lifted her up, and her legs wrapped around his waist. Finding her hands free, she wrapped her arms round his neck to bring him closer.

She rubbed her hips against him, enjoying the little thrills that shot up her spine as the friction hit just right against her clit through their clothes. His hands cupped her ass, bringing her forward onto the hard bulge growing in his pants.

"God ... need you ..." he groaned.

"Yes. *Now.*"

She wasn't sure what happened, but one moment he had her pinned to the door, and the next, she clung to him as he walked her inside Damon's office.

The loud thud of the door closing didn't even register in her brain as her body temperature rose, and that need to be with him, to have him inside her, eclipsed every other thought in her brain.

When he put her down, her hands fumbled at the buttons on his uniform shirt as his reached for the hem of her top. Their mouths only parted long enough for him to whip the sweater off her. She moaned when his hands found her breasts and cupped them through her bra, and she practically ripped the buttons off his shirt.

"Desk," she growled against his mouth. He didn't need to be told again as he lifted her up and crossed the room in half a second. She found herself planted on top of Damon's neat desk, knees parting to bring their hips back in contact. Though she protested when he pulled his mouth away, her body jolted when his lips landed on her neck. She thrust her fingers into his scalp, loosening the long hair tied back into a ponytail.

With a guttural grunt, he planted her down on the hard desk, stepping back, his breath coming in pants. The light outside was waning, casting shadows into the room from the trees outside, and her shifter senses adjusted as she traced her gaze up from his small waist, perfectly-formed abs exposed by his parted shirt and chiseled chest before landing on his face.

Wowza.

Her mate was eye-poppingly, panty-droppingly, *handsome.* Long, blond hair framed a face that would have made Lucifer jealous, with its patrician nose, cheekbones that could cut glass, and firm lips that were now swollen. When he took off his glasses, the naked desire in his blue-violet eyes could have made her spontaneously combust right then and there.

Awoooooooooga.

He pounced on her, reaching for her jeans and unzipping the fly. She eased her hips up to help him pull them off, dragging her panties along. Another guttural sound ripped from his mouth as he unbuckled his belt and pushed his pants down. One arm curled around her waist, bringing her closer to the edge of the desk. Her arms reached up to his shoulders, as he bent down and something blunt nudged at her entrance.

"Yes," she moaned against his ear. His cock pushed into her slick channel—Holy hell, she'd never been this wet before. Still, her eyes nearly rolled into the back of her skull as she felt his girth and length. *Whoa, cowboy!* She tugged at his scalp.

He must have sensed her discomfort because he stopped, letting her adjust. A few heartbeats later, she nudged at him, giving her hips an encouraging push, and he slowly began to enter her again. *Oh boy.* She was definitely going to walk funny tomorrow.

Arms came around her, hands clamping over her shoulders as he began to thrust into her. He buried his face in her neck, grunting and moaning against her as he sucked and grazed his teeth into her sensitive skin. Her body moved in time to his slow, languid thrusts, wanting more, but at the same time, wanting this to last.

Suddenly, a sound caught her sensitive feline hearing. Turning her head to the source, she found two familiar figures by the doorway, openly staring at them.

"Oh my God!" She made a motion to push him away, but his grip only tightened, and he gave her an indignant nip on the neck.

Neither Dutchy nor Krieger made a move as both of them continued to gawk. "You're still here? Were you raised in a barn?" So she grabbed the first thing she could—a stapler —and threw it at the couple. "Get out!"

Quickly, they turned around and left. *Perverts!* "Oh!" Holy shit, her mate didn't even flinch throughout the whole ordeal, but kept going at it. *What a champ!*

His thrusts sped up, and he brought her down on his cock, his fingers digging into her shoulders so hard she knew they would leave a mark. She clung to him, moving her hips in time to his until her body exploded with a quick and powerful orgasm.

She barely had time to recover when he pulled out of her, planted her feet on the ground, then flipped her body to bend her over the desk and kicked her legs apart.

Holy fuck! She had expected his cock to push back into her, but instead, she felt a warm, wet tongue lick at her pussy lips. The surprise coupled with the shock of feeling his mouth on her sent tingles of pleasure across her skin, and she found herself pushing against him, wanting more. There was something so carnal and dirty about not being able to see him, but only feel him and hear him eating her out that added excitement to this scenario.

A palm slipped under her belly and moved to her mound, fingers seeking her hardened clit. "Oh God!" Between his talented mouth and his wicked fingers, she came in half a second, her body vibrating against the great oak desk.

He shifted behind her again, his hands gripping her ass and giving it a squeeze before she felt his cock at her pussy again. *Oh Lord.* She couldn't remember calling on the Big Guy this much in her entire life, but if this wasn't a religious experience, she didn't know what was.

She braced herself against the table as he pounded hard into her. The steady oak table rocked under her, and she had to grip the edge to keep herself from slipping off. He was relentless, rutting fast into her, and as if he wasn't satisfied with how he filled her, hooked a hand under one of her legs to prop it up on the table so he could go even deeper.

"Yes, oh God, I'm coming!" she cried out as her body convulsed with another orgasm. Fingers dug into her hips as his thrusting became erratic, his cock pulsing inside her as he filled her with his warm seed. He let out a guttural cry, muttering words she couldn't make out as she was too busy riding out the wave of her own pleasure.

When her body finally stopped shaking, she plastered herself against the tabletop, her body sticky with sweat. He followed suit, pulling out before he collapsed on top of her, his chest heaving as his breath came in hard gasps before evening out.

Well, I guess this is where the awkwardness begins, she thought to herself. *Quick, say something to break the ice!*

And so, she said the first thing that came to her head. She reached behind her to raise her hand. "Great game, champ! High five!"

Chapter 2

As the sexual haze slowly cleared from his mind and the muscles in his body relaxed, the first thing that came to Dr. Cam Spenser's mind was, *Well, that was something.*

A mate. How fascinating.

As a man of science, the very idea of some kind of magical higher power controlling one's fate and choosing one's lifetime partner should have been horrifying to him. However, he couldn't say he was entirely opposed to the idea.

He'd heard stories and even met one or two colleagues who'd experienced the bond of fated mates, and it fascinated him on an intellectual level. Because surely, there was some kind of scientific explanation to the consuming need, overwhelming attraction, and urgency to procreate with just *one* particular person. Perhaps something in shifter physiology could detect the pheromones of the most ideal partner to breed with. Or maybe the correct combination of hormones and body chemistry set off some kind of reaction. A thorough study with subjects, experimentation, and trials could unlock the mystery behind mates and this pseudo-metaphysical bond that supposedly formed and linked their souls.

Of course, when he said all that aloud to his colleagues, they looked horrified and objected immediately. Cam didn't see what all the fuss was about—shifters were biological creatures after all, and he should know. He was one of them.

Yes, he'd always thought it was a shame mating and bonding was one of those things that shifters found so private that no one wanted to study it. *Think of the possibilities and applications,* he had told his colleagues. But none of them were persuaded, and they became even more outraged at the idea that something as "precious" and "sacred" as bonded mates could be put to the test of the scientific method. If Cam weren't already mired in the study of ecology and preservation, he would have considered pursuing such research. But now ...

His polar bear roared in protest.

Sharing his body with a wild beast could be an advantage at times, especially when conducting field work, but it could also be exasperating. Such as now, when the damned thing suddenly turned protective of their mate.

Their *mate.*

The awareness of the soft body beneath his jolted him. He blinked at the hand in front of his face.

"Uh, no high five then? How about—*oomph!*"

With his shifter speed, he slid off the table and dragged her up with him, flipping her over to face him. Those eyes—mostly light brown with large gray flecks—that entranced him the moment he'd seen them threatened to overwhelm him again.

Mine, his polar bear roared.

And her animal acknowledged it with a slow, languid, *mine*.

Despite the fact that his lust had been sated mere moments ago, he wanted her again. Wanted to be inside her. To feel her lips on his. Lick at her skin and—

"Whoa." She planted her hands on his chest. "Slow down, champ."

His cock bobbed painfully against her belly, and he took a step back. "P-pardon me," he said, clearing his throat. *For God's sake*, he scolded himself silently. *You're a grown man of thirty-six with two PhDs. Stop thinking with your damned cock for two seconds.*

He'd never lost control like he just had, but the moment their eyes met that first time, it was as if he lost his senses, and the only thing he knew was that he *had* to have her.

And now, the need continued to grow inside him—as did other parts—but, he let his logical, human side take over. *You can do this.* Straightening his shoulders, he cleared his throat. "My apologies, miss."

"I think we're way past formalities at this point, don't ya think?" A blonde brow raised at him. "But knowing your name might be nice."

"Right." He paused. "Um, I'm Cameron. Dr. Cameron Spenser. But you can call me Cam."

"I'm J.D. McNamara."

He frowned. "Like Jade with a y?"

"No, no. Like the letters." Holding her hands up, she shaped them with her fingers. "J. And D."

"Oh, I see." *Americans*, he grumbled silently. Whatever happened to good old-fashioned names like Linda or Anne or Emma? "It's, uh, lovely to meet you."

Those haunting eyes regarding him, the dominant colors shifting from light brown to steel gray before she burst out laughing. "That was one hell of an introduction, huh?"

Heat crept up his cheeks, and he ran his fingers through his hair. "I didn't mean to ... I mean, obviously I did, but ..." Cam had always prided himself on his control and discipline. He had learned from a young age to control his polar bear all on his own. After all, Mum had died young before she was able to pass the lessons shifter parents were supposed to teach their young. And his father? Well—

"It's all right, I was kidding. What? You don't get jokes where you're from?" Her pert little nose wrinkled. "Say ... where're you from, anyway?"

"Surrey. In England."

"Oh, like London?"

He wanted to roll his eyes, but tamped down the urge. Of course, Americans only knew of London whenever England was mentioned. His polar bear slashed at him, as if warning him not to be rude to their mate. *Like I would ever*. "Yes, just outside London," he said, using his standard answer.

"Oh, cool. You have such a sexy accent," she purred.

Normally, commenting on his accent was another thing that irritated him about the people of this country, but coming from her, he felt enormously flattered, especially when she looked at him with such naked desire. But speaking of naked ... "Um, perhaps we should get dressed? And leave before the chief comes back?" Bloody hell, did they really have sex in his boss's office? Damon was going to have his hide.

"Comes back?" She guffawed. "Unlikely, but yeah, we should probably get dressed." Bending down, she picked up her discarded trousers. He couldn't help but watch her shapely backside and her skin that seemed to glow in the moonlight.

"I did notice it was empty and dark in the building." He glanced around and found his own khaki uniform pants and hopped into them. "Damon usually works until seven. I was hoping to catch him before he left, but that's when I ran into you." What was she doing in here? She wasn't a ranger or employee; he certainly would have recognized her weeks ago if that was the case.

"Well, yeah," she chuckled. "It's Thanksgiving."

"Thanksgiving?"

"Yeah. You know. Turkey. Stuffing. Football and—oh!" Realization dawned on her face. "Of course you wouldn't know. You're not American."

"I know about Thanksgiving," he countered. Still, that was today? "But it's only Wednesday."

"Yeah, but today is the Blackstone Rangers Thanksgiving party." She dashed toward the door and grabbed something from the floor—her hat and jumper he'd discarded earlier. "You're a ranger, right?" Shaking it off, she slipped the top over, then her head popped out from the neck. He noticed tattoos down her left arm, but before he could make out what they were, she had tucked it under the sleeve. "Didn't anyone invite you?" Combing her hair with her fingers, she pushed her blonde curls under the hat.

He picked up his shirt from the floor and slipped it on. "I'm ... not sure."

Technically he was part of the Blackstone Rangers, and he did his shifts and duties as required. However, he preferred to keep to himself and didn't socialize with any of the other rangers or employees because he couldn't afford to be distracted. After all, he didn't move to a different continent to make friends. As one of the largest, privately-owned preserves in the United States, the ecology in the Blackstone Mountains was lush and nearly pristine. No one had yet done any research in the area. This was a chance afforded to no one else, and he couldn't get distracted. Especially not with such a limited timetable.

"Hello? Cam?" She waved a hand at him.

"Yes. Damon did mention something the other day, if I recall correctly." Initially, Cam didn't think Damon would be interested in his scientific work, but he was taken by surprise. Damon sought him out every now and then and liked to hear his findings, and once in a while even asked his opinions about how they could improve with their operations and conservation efforts. That had earned Damon his respect and admiration. "However, I didn't realize that was this week." He finished buttoning up his uniform shirt and took his glasses out of the front shirt pocket.

She raised a brow. "Do you even need those? I mean, I'm digging the sexy professor look, but you're a shifter, right? A ... bear?"

"I don't," he said. Shifters had enhanced senses after all, but he'd had them for a long time now. *Keep those on, Cameron,* his father had instructed when he dropped him off at boarding school. *They make you look more human and normal.* Swallowing the unexpected lump in his throat, he added, "And, yes. Polar bear, actually."

"You're shitting me!" she exclaimed excitedly. "Like for real?"

"Of course, why would I lie?"

Her hands clapped together. "Polar—oh my God, you really are my mate." She hugged him and squeezed tight. "I can't believe ... oh the guys will never—" Her arms dropped to her sides, and she stepped back. "Wait—we are mates, right?"

"Yes." His bear did not like the way she shrank back apprehensively. And neither did he. What could she be thinking?

"And that means ... you and I ..." She gestured between them. "I mean, are you going to ... we should ..."

"We should what?" he asked, exasperated. "Spit it out, will you?"

Her hands curled at her sides. "You're not going to fight it, are you?"

"Why the bloody hell would I do that?" His bear, too, roared in defiance.

Her jaw dropped, then her shoulders relaxed. "Oh. Thank God. I thought you were having some kind of post-nut clarity, and you realized you didn't want this."

"Post-nut ... what do you mean?"

"I've seen this dance before. My friends, well most of them anyway, they had their reasons for not wanting to be with their mates and made up all kinds of excuses when it's obvious to everyone they're right for each other."

"That seems illogical." This was biology they were talking about. If something—whether pheromones or chemistry or shifter physiology—had deemed them compatible, then why should they ignore it? His bear agreed heartily. "It's in our nature. Our instinct. We couldn't possibly defy it any more than newly-hatched sea turtles stop themselves from crawling into the sea." Besides, it was an interesting prospect. To be able to discover and observe the mating of shifters firsthand would be a fascinating thing indeed.

Her hands planted on her hips. "Did you just compare me to a *sea turtle*?"

"I, uh ..." He never was good with women, unfortunately. While they were initially attracted to him for whatever reason, it was difficult to figure out what things to say that wouldn't make them angry. Or vexed. Or generally annoyed. So, he just kept silent most of the time. It seemed easier, so as not to dig himself into a bigger hole. "It's not that—"

"Because sea turtles are adorable," she finished with a laugh.

He relaxed. "Yes, they are." And now his curiosity was piqued—what was she? Was he supposed to know already? He remembered trace scents of fur, but he'd been distracted by ... other parts of her. His gaze lowered to her lips, and he took a step forward, hands reaching out. "J.D. ..."

"Yes?" Her lips parted, her voice low and husky.

Christ, he wanted her again. And again. This new sensation of lust and want was exhilarating, but also distracting. But he had to control himself, even though he could already smell her arousal, along with the sweet, female scent. "I think we should ... explore this ... between us."

Her hands planted on his chest as her eyes darkened. "Oh, I agree ... we definitely should explore."

"And do things the right way."

"You've definitely done things the right way." Moving closer to him, she pressed her body up against his. "But I'm open to trying other things too."

"I ..." His cock twitched in his pants. But his own learned

instinct from his human side quickly fought to shut down his need. "What I mean is ... perhaps we should slow down."

"Slow down? Didja want me to buy you some flowers or something? Ask your father for permission to take you out?"

He snorted. Like his father would have given a damn—oh. *It was another joke.* "No, not at all." He pushed his glasses up his nose by habit. "What I meant is, perhaps we can get to know each other. Spend more time together before we ... uh ... again ..."

Hazel eyes narrowed at him. "Before we what?"

"You know." He harrumphed. "Do I have to spell it out?"

"Ohhh. You mean, take a one-way ride to pound town? Make the beast with two backs? Do the bedroom rodeo? Burp the worm—"

"Yes," he interrupted. "Don't get me wrong, J.D., I enjoyed what transpired between us."

"But you don't want to do it again?" Confusion and hurt crossed her face.

"I do." Bloody hell, if she only knew how much, she'd probably run in the opposite direction. "But this is all new to me. And to you, too, I imagine."

"Yeah ... I don't do this kind of thing, just so you know."

Not knowing what else to say, he decided to just tell her the truth. "It's overwhelming, and I ... I don't want to make a mistake."

Her hazel eyes looked up at him. "That's so ... so sweet of you."

"I want to do this the proper way."

"I guess that makes sense. When my friends talk about the bond, they say it's something special, but we have to be open to it if we want it to form."

A sudden, inexplicable fear gripped him. What if this didn't work out with J.D.? Their animal sides were in tune, but what if their human sides didn't get along? Could they just go their separate ways? Form relationships with other people? His bear didn't like that one bit.

"I wish I could peek into that mind of yours," she said slyly. "What's going on? What's wrong?"

"Nothing," he said, brushing those thoughts away. He knew he had a tendency to overthink things, but talking to himself helped assess any situation. Most people mistook his silence for coldness or indifference which made it difficult for him to act normally in social situations. He'd been like that most of his life, preferring his inner musings. His father's voice broke into his thoughts from out of nowhere. *Why can't you just act* normal, *Cameron?*

She crossed her arms over her chest. "Wait, are you trying to tell me you want to start dating first?"

"Yes, exactly."

"Huh." She tapped a finger on her chin. "It wasn't what I was expecting, but I suppose we could give it a try."

He breathed a sigh of relief. "Good."

"So." She placed her hands on her hips. "Are there gonna be rules? Like only up to second base until the third date?"

"I, uh ... how about we just play it by ear? But of course, I would respect your boundaries and your limits."

She burst out laughing. "If we respected my boundaries, we'd be horizontal right now."

A fresh surge of lust rose in him. "You're trying my patience, love," he warned.

"Oh yeah?" The corners of her lips turned up. "I'd try more than your patience. Whatcha gonna do about it?" Her fingers walked up his chest. "Are you gonna spank me, Dr. Spenser?"

Bloody hell. He wrapped his hand around her wrist and brought her closer. The fire in her eyes emboldened him. "Perhaps I will, if you continue to be a naughty girl."

"Oh geez," she groaned, taking a step back. "C'mon, Christian Grey, let's get outta here. You're making my kitty all riled up. And I'm not talking about my inner animal."

When Damon had mentioned there would be some kind of party, Cam hadn't quite expected such an elaborate affair. The normally bare dining hall had been done up in brilliant autumn colors and fall-themed decor. It was also packed with people, and not just the rangers and employees. There were many faces he didn't recognize and several children running around and screaming like banshees.

"Oh, they already started!" J.D. exclaimed as they walked through the door. "Let's go to our table."

"Our table?" Perhaps he should have thought this part through. He didn't even know who J.D. McNamara was exactly and how she came to be here. Was she someone's daughter or sister?

She dragged him along, waving and chatting to several people, many of them his workmates. It was almost comical the way their faces cheered up when they looked at her, and then turned confused or downright unpleasant when their gazes turned to him. To say that he hadn't made many good impressions around here was an understatement, but he was never really good at small talk or congeniality. He tended to be too direct and stiff, especially around gregarious and overly-friendly Americans.

But she didn't seem to mind, and now that they were under better light, he couldn't help but stare down at her.

Objectively speaking, J.D. was attractive. Blonde. Hazel eyes. Slim build with the right amount of curves. Who wouldn't give her a second glance?

But un-objectively speaking? She was the most exquisite creature he'd laid eyes on. The tendrils of hair coming loose from under her hat were the color of wheat. She had a pert nose, clear, milky skin, and thick blonde lashes framing her unusual eyes. Eyes that were now looking up at him, amused.

"Something the matter?"

"Uh, no," he said quickly, realizing he'd been caught. "Apologies. I didn't mean to stare."

"You can stare all you want, champ," she purred. "No one'll make a fuss. Me least of all."

"J.D.!" a feminine voice called them. "Where have you been?"

"Uh, busy." They stopped in front of a pretty blonde woman. "Hey, Anna Victoria, have you met Cam? Cam Spenser?"

Cam recognized the woman as Anna Victoria Cooper, Damon's mate and wife. "Why yes, we met briefly at the Blackstone Rangers anniversary ball," she said. "Nice to see you again, Dr. Spenser." Her gaze zeroed in on him, then down to their linked hands, then back up to his face. She lifted a brow at J.D. "And how are you two acquainted?"

J.D. gave a nervous laugh. "Funny you should ask—"

"Where'd you go off to, J.D?" A man with dark blond hair came up from behind Anna Victoria. "I thought you'd be the first one lining up for the turkey. Oh, hey." Friendly blue eyes regarded him. "Have we met? Gabriel Russel."

Gabriel seemed familiar, then Cam recalled he'd been on the other side of their table during the Blackstone Rangers ball. He offered his hand anyway. "I think we did meet briefly at the ball as well. But it's nice to meet your acquaintance again. Dr. Cameron Spenser."

"Right. You're the doctor who took my place on the roster," he said, taking the hand Cam held out. "Hope the job's treating you well. Are you—" He stopped short when he noticed he and J.D. were holding hands. Instead of releasing his grip, Gabriel tightened it. "So, Doc, how exactly do you and our dear old J.D. know each other?"

Our J.D.? His bear did not like that possessive word one bit, and so he returned the shake with equal strength and positioned himself between Gabriel and his mate.

"Oh please." J.D. rolled her eyes. "Drag your knuckles off the ground and quit with the male posturing shit. Cam is—"

"Anna Victoria, I thought you were just going to get dessert?" Damon said as he sidled up to his wife.

Cam mentally slapped his head. *Perhaps I should have thought this through.* "Chief," he greeted his boss tersely.

"Cam?" Damon looked as if Cam had grown a second head. "You decided to join us for this all-American tradition after all. Did you—" His jaw tensed and brows furrowed as his green gaze ping-ponged between Cam and Gabriel, whose hands remained locked in a death grip. "Somebody want to explain?"

Gabriel huffed. "Yeah, somebody better."

Cam's head snapped toward Gabriel, noting the way the other man's jaw hardened and his gaze blazed. Who was this male? And why was he being overprotective of *his* mate? His bear let its disapproval known with a growl. It was answered with an equally fierce roar from the other man's animal.

Damon stepped in front of them. "Let. Go." The dominant force of his Kodiak bear cowered both his and Gabriel's animals, and they both released each other at the same time.

Damon crossed his arms over his chest. "Explain."

"Oh, for fuck's sake. Relax, guys." J.D. scrubbed a palm down her face. "Cam is my mate."

Three jaws simultaneously dropped.

"Mate?" Anna Victoria said, breathless. "J.D. that's wonderful!" She pulled J.D. in for a hug, and since the blonde was already mated, Cam allowed it.

"You're mates?" Gabriel looked utterly stunned. "Holy shit, McNamara!" he laughed, and the tension broke in the air. "Congratulations." Then he turned to Cam and mouthed, *I'm sorry.*

"Hey!" J.D. protested. "I saw that."

"Congratulations, both of you," Damon said, clapping him on the back. "I ... can't say I expected this. But, I'm glad for you both. Finding your mate is a special thing." He wrapped an arm around Anna Victoria and smiled at her, perhaps the first time Cam had ever seen Damon show any tender emotion.

"Uh, thank you." He was still confused about something. "But if you don't mind ... how do you all know each other?"

"Damon and Gabriel have been my best friends since grade school," J.D. explained. "We're practically family."

"I see."

"Yeah, we're basically her brothers." Gabriel puffed up

his chest. "While he was around, her Pop always told us to look out for her," he added. Though the chief didn't say anything, Damon's protective glare stared a hole into him.

"Gabriel, Damon," J.D. began. "Be nice. Please."

"What are your intentions toward her?" Damon asked. "Are you going to play around with her? Do you intend to claim her?"

"Oh, ha! That's rich coming from you," Anna Victoria interjected, tugging at her mate's arm. "You didn't want to claim me and even went out of your way to be nasty and push me away."

"That's different," he said, which only got him a chilly stare from his wife.

"Well, he better," Gabriel said. "But if you're not gonna treat her right—"

"Guys, put your dicks aside, all right?" J.D. said in an exasperated tone. "Cam and I have decided that we're going to take things slow and get to know each other."

"Wow," Gabriel said. "That actually sounds ... sensible. So unlike you."

"Hey!"

Anna Victoria cleared her throat. "Now that we have that out of the way, why don't you two get some food and then join us at our table?"

"Sounds like a plan." J.D. tugged on his hand. "C'mon, champ, let's get you a plate. You've never had a traditional Thanksgiving feast before, have you?"

"Can't say I have."

"Great! I'll help you pile your plate." She turned to the trio. "We'll be right back."

Chapter 3

Despite his initial reservations, Cam actually found himself enjoying the festivities. Perhaps he suddenly felt some kind of holiday spirit or it was being around his mate. He suspected it was the latter because growing up, his holidays were nothing like this.

Are your mummy and daddy picking you up, Cam?

What are you eating on Christmas Day, Cam? My mum's making my favorite mince pie!

Dad's getting me the newest video game console. What's your dad getting you, Cam?

Each year, the endless questions went on and on from the other boys at St. Andrews when everyone was preparing to go home at the end of the term. And each year, he couldn't come up with any answer.

"Where'd you go off to?" J.D. asked as she waved her hand in front of him. "Are you getting sleepy already? That's the tryptophan working."

"What?" He blinked, finding himself transported back to the present. "You know that's not true, right? They've disproven that turkey makes you sleepy. Unless you eat copious amounts—"

She shoved a forkful of mashed potatoes into his mouth. "Here, have these before you make me swoon with your sexy talk."

As she promised, J.D. filled his plate high with turkey, stuffing, and other sides, and they sat down to eat with Damon, Anna Victoria, Gabriel, and his mate, Temperance. The food was delicious, if a little too greasy and rich. When he commented on it, his mate merely snorted. "That's what the holidays are for!"

"Hey, has anyone seen Dutchy and Krieger?" Anna Victoria asked. "Did they leave for the airport already? I know they didn't want to get caught up in the traffic and crowds."

"I have," J.D. said, raising a hand. "We ran into them. Or rather, they ran into us."

"They did?" Cam frowned. He didn't recall seeing anyone else.

"Yeah, while we were in Damon's off—oops!" She looked guiltily at Damon, then turned away.

"While you were in Damon's *what*?" the chief asked, his brows furrowing together.

"Uh ..." J.D. raised a spoonful of mashed potatoes to her mouth and mumbled, "Nothing."

"J.D..." Damon warned.

J.D. swallowed. "Uh, so I went into your office and raided your candy bar drawer."

A vein popped out in Damon's forehead. "You stole my peanut butter cups, didn't you?"

"I was hungry!" she pouted.

"And then what?"

"I was coming out and I bumped into Cam, and we realized we were mates ... and then one thing led to another, and Dutchy and Krieger walked in—"

"Hold on a moment," Cam said. "Two people walked in on us? Why did I not notice?"

"You were *distracted*." J.D. winked at him.

"J.D.!" Damon exclaimed loudly. "What the hell? In my office?"

"On your desk, actually," she said proudly, then turned to Anna Victoria. "You were right. It *is* the perfect height."

The vein on the chief's head throbbed. "You *told* her?"

"What?" Anna Victoria said. "She plied me with wine, and you know how I get when I have too much chardonnay."

"Don't worry." J.D. waved a hand. "The cleaning crew will clean everything up before you get there on Monday. Besides, from what else Anna Victoria told me, they should be used to it."

Anna Victoria looked sheepishly at her mate, who looked like he was about to explode.

"Ha! I knew you guys were getting freaky in there," Gabriel said, holding his hand up. "High five, Chief."

Damon glared at him, which made the other man lower his hand.

"My, uh, apologies, Damon," Cam managed to say. This was not only embarrassing, but inappropriate conversation in public. "I swear it won't happen again."

"It better not," he muttered.

"Hey, guys," someone said as they came up from behind them. "We're heading home, Darcey's pretty tired with the baby and all."

"Yeah, I think it's the tryptophan," a feminine voice added.

Bugger. As if his evening couldn't get any worse, he realized who had come up to say goodbye—Darcey Wednesday. And *Anders Stevens*.

Darcey walked around the table to where Anna Victoria was sitting to give her a hug. "Happy Thanksgiving—Cam?" she said when her gaze landed on him. "Oh, Cam, nice to see you. How have you been?"

"You look well, Darcey," he said.

The tension in the air grew as Anders came to stand beside her, his arm going around her shoulders protectively. "Look who came down from his high and mighty tower to join us peasants."

"Anders," Damon said in a warning tone.

"What?" The tiger shifter shrugged. "Didn't think you'd be the type to show up to these things. Thank you for gracing us with your presence," he sneered.

"Hey, Stevens," J.D. began. "I heard there's a land called Douche-istan looking for a king. Should I tell them the search is over?"

Anders turned to J.D. "You're defending this guy now?"

"Defend?" J.D. asked. "What did he ever do to you?"

Bloody hell. This was not how Cam wanted this conversation to go. If only pesky little things like the laws of physics didn't prevent him from traveling back in time to tell J.D. why Anders hated him before all this. Or stop him from asking Darcey out on a date in the first place.

Thankfully, Gabriel shot up to his feet and spoke up. "Anders, Darcey, I need to talk to you guys about … something."

"What about, Gabriel?" Darcey asked.

Gabriel looked to his fiancé. Temperance immediately got up as well. "Uh, shower curtains."

"Shower curtains?" Darcey looked confused.

Temperance came over to her side and looped her hand through her arm. "Yeah. I need your opinion about which ones to get for our bathroom. Right, Gabriel?"

"Definitely." Gabriel took Anders by the arm and dragged him away, with Temperance and Darcey following suit.

J.D.'s expression was that of pure confusion. "Am I missing something here?"

Anna Victoria cleared her throat. "We should go get more pie."

"Right," Damon added, helping Anna Victoria up. "Um, maybe we'll see you around, Cam," he said before they walked away.

Now that they were alone, J.D. crossed her arms over her chest and turned to him. "Well?"

What could he possibly say that wouldn't end up with J.D. walking away or slapping him? This was why he avoided interpersonal relationships with the opposite sex. Apparently, he was terrible with women. "I didn't get a chance to tell you this because I wasn't expecting to run into Darcey and Anders. In fact, I'd successfully avoided them these past months and—"

"Just spit it out."

He huffed out a breath. "Darcey and I used to date—I mean, we went out on dates."

Confusion, then hurt, crossed his mate's face. Her

animal, on the other hand, hissed at him. "You and Darcey?" she said in a quiet voice.

His bear roared in outrage. "Bloody hell." He massaged his temples with his fingers. "It's not like that. I mean ... we went out on three dates. That's it. The last one was the Blackstone Rangers ball, and after that, she told me she didn't have any feelings for me. And frankly ... it was a relief. I didn't feel any attraction toward her."

"Relief?" she echoed. "Why did you ask her out in the first place, then?"

How could he explain it best without sounding like a cold bastard or awkward nutter? "J.D., love." He took her hands into his. She stiffened at the contact, which made his chest twinge, but at least she didn't pull away. "In case you didn't notice. People here ... they don't like me very much." Actually, it wasn't just here; he'd always been a loner. There was no need to develop social skills if one didn't socialize, and that was the way he preferred it. At least until this very moment.

"What?"

"I have this reputation, and I put people off because I say what's on my mind, and that's after I've already debated with myself on the subject. And Darcey ... well, we bumped into each other in a coffee shop, and she'd left her wallet at home, so I offered to pay. In that instance, I was ... a sort of hero for her, and it made things less awkward, I think. She didn't know who I was and she was charming and lovely—her personality I mean," he clarified. "I felt at ease around her, perhaps it was because she was a shifter or because she was also new to Blackstone and living around so many like us for the first time. So, I thought I would ask her out, and we went on two dinner dates.

And then Damon told me I had to show up at this damned ball, and so naturally, I asked her to come. She and Anders had already met, and I had no idea they were mates. I even accompanied her to drinks with a colleague, but only as friends. I felt responsible, and it turns out I *was* responsible—for getting her kidnapped."

"Wait, a minute. You had something to do with that?"

"In a way. I introduced her to the man who connected her with the Alpha who abducted her," he said.

"Oh."

"Anyway, you know the story after that. And a few weeks ago, Darcey told me the news that she was mated and expecting Anders's child." To be frank, that had been a relief to hear too. "So, it's understandable that Anders feels some anger and resentment toward me. I did inadvertently put his mate and child in danger."

J.D.'s lips pursed, and her brows narrowed. *Here we go*, he thought to himself. She was angry at him, obviously, for dating one of her friends. "J.D.? Will you say something, please?"

She gritted her teeth together. "First of all, it's not your fault that Darcey was kidnapped, it was that asshole fake Alpha who wanted her gone." Her fingers gripped his tightly. "And second, if no one likes you because you speak your mind, they can fuck right the fuck off this planet."

"I—what?" He stared at her, dumbfounded. Did she just *defend* him?

"And by the way, if you didn't introduce Darcey to that guy, then she wouldn't have found her biological family in

Australia," she pointed out. "She and Anders got back from their trip to Perth a few days ago. Got engaged too."

"Wait a minute," he said. "You're not angry with me?"

"For what?"

"You know ... Darcey and I."

She pursed her lips. "Did anything happen?"

"Absolutely not. We've never shared more than a friendly hug," he said.

"All right then." She patted him on the shoulder. "We're good."

Cam didn't move an inch, still not quite believing what had happened. "Thank you. I was afraid you'd burst into some kind of jealous tirade and storm off." He hated showing petty feelings like jealousy or envy. They were irrational and unnecessary.

"I'm not upset because you went out with Darcey," she began. "You both were single and free, and though a tiny—a teeny tiny—part of me *is* jealous, that happened before we even met. I was just caught off guard because everyone knew before I did, and I hated that feeling."

"Of course, I understand." She'd been humiliated, and that was after she'd defended him. "And I'm sorry if you were hurt."

"Thank you. I mean, it's no one's fault. It's not like we had time to discuss our past. I mean, we only had our meet-cute what, over an hour ago?"

"Meet what?"

"You *know*," she nudged him with her elbow. "Our meet-cute. The cute story we're going to tell everyone when they ask how we met. Or is it meet-sex in this case?" She shook her head. "Anyway, maybe you're right. About the going slow thing. I just ... I don't wanna fuck this up, Cam."

The sincerity in her voice made his heart twitch. "You won't ... I mean, we won't," he reassured her.

"Good." She grinned up at him. "Actually, I just realized something hilarious."

He caressed the side of her face. "And what's that?"

"Anders asked me to the same shindig," she said with a chuckle. "Can you imagine if I had shown up on his arm at the ball?"

"What?" A strange, tight ball curled up in his chest. "He asked you out? On a *date*?"

"Only because he had no one else. And I said no, obviously. But what if I did come and we met and—" Her brows knitted together. "Wait ... are *you* jealous?"

"Jealous?" His voice pitching higher than he expected. "I do *not* get jealous." His bear, on the other hand, begged to disagree. *Oh, shut up.*

"Uh-huh." The corners of her lips tugged up. "Anyway ... can we move on? Fresh start?"

The idea of J.D. and Anders going to that ball was still making his head buzz, but he swallowed those unnamed emotions. "All right. How about we get some dessert?"

The rest of the evening proceeded with much less excitement. Damon, Anna Victoria, Gabriel, and Temperance came back, and they were also joined by Daniel Rogers and his mate, Sarah and her brother Adam. There was no more talk of the past, and Cam found himself at ease.

When things finally wound down, he escorted J.D. back to her truck in the parking lot.

"You got a ride home?" she asked as she unlocked her door.

"Yes." He nodded to the dark blue Range Rover on the other side of the lot. "I'm renting a flat in South Blackstone, though I'm hardly there. With work and my research taking up a lot of my time, most nights I just nap in one of the dorm beds, especially after a night shift. But since the offices will be closed down for the holiday, I suppose I'll have to go home."

"Right." Turning around, she faced him and placed her hand on his chest. "So ... are we still doing this going slow thing?"

"Of course." He cupped her face with both hands, thumbs caressing her cheeks, and stared down into those marvelous eyes of her. "I want to get to know you better."

Her lids lowered, her lashes casting shadows over her cheekbones. "What do you want to know?" she asked in a low, sensuous tone.

"For one thing ..." He lowered his head toward hers. "What does J.D. stand for?"

"Whoa." She pressed her palms firmly on his shoulders. "I thought we were slowing down."

"What's wrong with your real name?"

"Nothing," she said. "It's just ... I'll tell you some other time, okay? When I'm ready."

"Fine. But how about you tell me what your animal is." His bear, too, was itching to know.

She took a step back. "I said slow down, not put it on light speed there, champ."

He frowned. "So, you won't tell me your real name or your animal? Is there something the matter?"

"No, it's ... it's silly," she said. "But maybe it could be part of the process. Of how we get to know each other. It'll keep things exciting."

He supposed that made sense. While their animals knew they were mates, their human sides needed to catch up. That's what this was about, right? "All right."

"So, speaking of which ... what do you have planned for tomorrow?"

"Me?" He paused. "Nothing. I suppose I could finish up some paperwork—"

"What?" She sounded offended, as if he'd insulted her grandmother. "Nuh-uh. Tomorrow is Thanksgiving, and you're not working."

"I'm not?"

"No. You're coming with me to spend the day with Damon and Gabriel."

"I don't think—"

"Oh c'mon, Cam. Please?" She batted her eyelashes at him. "Damon and Gabriel are like my family. I mean, no. They *are* my family. If you want us to work out, you're going to have to get along with them."

"All right," he relented. "But if I agree, can I ask for one thing in return?"

"Anything. What is it?"

"How about a goodnight kiss?"

She chuckled. "Like I would let you leave without kissing me."

"I—*mmm!*"

J.D. practically attacked him, her arms going around his neck and pulling him down to meet her lush mouth. Once again, pure lust and need surged in him as he devoured her sweet lips. He got lost in her—her scent, her taste, her very being, that before he knew it, he had her pinned against the side of her truck, her legs wrapped around him, and his hands under her bra, teasing her nipples.

"Ah ... Cam!" Her hips rocked against his growing erection. Her overpowering scent set his blood on fire, and he didn't care they were outside. He wanted her, to be inside her again and feel her squeezing—

The sound of a car starting a few rows away from them snapped him back to his senses, and he pulled away. She whimpered in protest.

Calm yourself, Cameron, he scolded himself. And so, he set her down on the ground. "Uh, apologies."

"Don't be sorry for that," she said wryly. "Or *that*."

He followed her gaze to where his hands were still under her top. His only regret was that he had been so consumed by the need to have her when they met that he didn't get a chance to see her fully naked body or her breasts. Even now, her nipples were like hard pebbles between his fingers, and he wondered what they tasted like.

"Oh ... I ..." He quickly pulled his hands away and pulled down her jumper. "I'm—what the hell?" He blinked as he noticed the design knitted into her top and began to read it aloud. "'I like big—' Have you been wearing that the entire time?"

"Yeah. It's my favorite Thanksgiving sweater." With a great big sigh, she laid her head against his chest. "Are you sure I can't convince you to come over for a sleepover? I promise we can keep it PG."

He wrapped his arms around her and buried his nose in her hair, taking a deep whiff of her scent. "You might be able to promise that, but I can't." He knew if they were ever alone again, he wouldn't be able to stop himself. Nor would he want to. It was strange and irrational this need to claim her and make her his. But once he got caught up in it, it was the only thing he could think of.

Another thought struck him in that moment. "By the way, J.D., I should have addressed this as soon as we, uh, finished, but if there is a child, I would take responsibility—"

"Whoa, hold on!" A panicked look struck her face and she held her hands out. "There could be that, but you don't have to worry. My heat suppressants come with a healthy dose of shifter-strength birth control," she chortled. "So, no bun in this oven anytime soon."

Huh. Heat suppressants. J.D. was feline then, as only the female of her species of shifters experienced heat cycles.

"All right, now that we have that awkward conversation out of the way," she said, taking a step back. "How about you come to my place around noon, and we can ride up to Damon's together? I'll text you the address." They had exchanged numbers earlier in the evening.

"Sound like a plan." He shoved his hands in his pockets. "Drive safe, J.D. Please let me know when you get home safe." While his bear wanted him to follow her and make sure of that himself, he refused to give in as he wouldn't be able to stop himself from taking her up on her offer for a sleepover. *We need to do this right*, he told his grumpy bear.

She climbed into her truck, closed the door, then stuck her head out the window as she started the engine. Flashing him a saucy grin, she waved and pulled out of the space. He took a step back and returned her wave, watching the truck as it left the parking lot and then turned down the road, disappearing into the distance.

A void opened up in his chest at the realization he was alone, which was then filled with regret. Should he have taken her up on her offer? Did it really matter since they'd already been intimate?

His bear, of course, wanted to be with her. It pressed its giant white furry paws against his chest, as if trying to get him to let it out so he could go after J.D.

Absolutely not, he told the creature. *Just be patient.*

It pouted at him and sulked in the corner.

It was only rational and logical that he should get to know her first. And that she get to know him. The real him.

From out of nowhere, a deep-seated fear gripped him at the realization. To quote his mate, he didn't want to 'fuck this up' either. But there were so many things J.D. didn't know about him.

And what she did know wasn't even the tip of the proverbial iceberg. Underneath the surface was a continent-sized jumble of personal, not to mention *familial,* issues she had no clue about.

Had he forgotten about what he left behind? His duties and his history? Just because he'd crossed the Atlantic, it didn't mean they didn't exist. If—no, when—she did find out, well ...

He would have to ease her into it, and just hope and pray that it wouldn't send her running in the opposite direction.

Chapter 4

J.D. hummed to herself as she waited for noon to roll around the next day. Damon had said it was fine to bring Cam along, of course. Not that she would have cared either way, because she probably would have bullied or blackmailed him if he'd said the opposite or ask the real boss, AKA Anna Victoria, for permission.

As she sat on the couch fiddling with her phone, a notification popped up indicating she had gotten a text message. A groan escaped her mouth when she saw the name.

Roy Jorell.

The message summary began with, *Happy Turkey Day! What are you....*

Ugh. He was the last person she wanted to think about right now. But before she could swipe it away, a phone call came in. Her heart sped up, wondering if it was Cam, but another name flashed on the caller ID, one that made her pause before taking it. "Darcey?"

"H-hey, J.D." The swan shifter sounded just as surprised. "Happy Thanksgiving."

"Happy Thanksgiving," she said. "What's up? How've you been?"

"I'm good." There was a pause. "I know this is out of blue. Me calling you that is. And I wasn't sure if you wanted to talk to me, but I wanted to say sorry about last night."

"Sorry? Hun, whaddaya got to be sorry about? If anything, it should be Anders apologizing." She still didn't like the way Anders spoke to Cam. Her cat, too, wanted to reach out and swipe at him.

"Yes, that too. I'll talk to him about that." Her tone turned somber. "I mean, I'm sorry I didn't tell you about Cam and me. Gabriel explained that you and Cam were mates, and if I had known—"

"Hold on, Darce," she interrupted. "There's nothing for you to apologize for. It was in the past, before he and I met. And it's not like I was waiting around for him to come along."

"I know. But you looked so pissed last night."

"Only because I was blindsided. Everyone seemed to know that you and Cam went out except me. And really, I don't have any right to complain; Cam and I only met an hour before that, so it's not like we had time to talk about who we dated in the past. So please, Darcey, don't feel bad at all. I don't want things to be awkward between us, because I consider you a good friend. One of the few female friends I have."

"Oh, J.D., you don't know how happy that makes me." She sniffled. "Sorry. Pregnancy hormones."

"Don't worry about it. How are you feeling, by the way? And tell me all about your trip and meeting your family."

They chatted for a few more minutes until she heard the sound of a Range Rover stopping outside her door. "Uh, listen, I gotta go, Darce. I'll see you sometime, okay?"

"Sure! Why don't you stop by the shop next week? Maybe you can pick out a present to unwrap for Cam for Christmas."

Darcey, along with her adoptive sister Sarah, ran Blackstone's only lingerie shop, Silk, Lace, and Whispers. "Ooh! I like that idea. I'll definitely come by." After saying goodbye to Darcey and hanging up, she bounded toward the door, opening it before Cam could knock.

It was twelve on the dot, and he was already standing there, one hand raised halfway. The sight of him and the sheer force of the attraction she felt made her want to get down on her knees to thank whichever god had sent him as her mate. "Hey, Cam," she greeted, trying to sound casual and not too pathetic.

Those smoldering blue-violet eyes drilled right into her. "Good morning, love."

She braced herself against the door to keep from melting into a pool of mush. That sexy voice and yummy accent was too much. "Don't you look nice," she commented.

His hair was tied back, and he had his usual gold-rimmed glasses on, but instead of the khaki rangers uniform, he wore a blue sweater over a white collared shirt, jeans, and boots. A leather jacket was slung casually over his shoulder. Did nothing look terrible on this man?

His face lit up. "So do"—his gaze dropped down to her chest—"uh, you."

"It's my second favorite Thanksgiving sweater," she said

proudly. "Like it?" There was a cartoon turkey on the front, and underneath it said "Pluck me."

"It's ... interesting."

"No need to be polite. Tell me what you really think about it."

"Is this a trick question?"

She chuckled. "I promise I won't get mad."

He shook his head. "What is with you and these ridiculous jumpers?"

"It's my way of getting into the holiday spirit. Don't you—oh!" She gasped when she found herself pinned up against the doorframe and Cam's arms wound around her. Before she could protest, his mouth descended on hers, and she really almost did melt into a puddle at his feet.

His lips were warm and surprisingly soft, and though he was more subdued today, it didn't lessen the desire zinging through her system. When his hand shoved into her hair and pulled back, she found herself opening up to him, welcoming his tongue into her mouth. His scent, his *everything* was just so overwhelming, and she was tempted to pull him in and drag him by the hair to her bedroom. As if by mutual agreement, they released each other at the same time.

"Sorry ... I, uh ..."

"Your glasses are fogged up," she said with a giggle.

"Ah, yes." He quickly took them off and wiped them on his sweater.

J.D. wasn't sure why he wore them in the first place, and she didn't miss how he evaded that question last night. *Who are you, Dr. Cameron Spenser?* she wondered.

As much as she was suffering from a case of lady blue balls, she couldn't disagree with his sound logic about not sleeping together again. The sex had been out of this world, which made it distracting. They hardly knew each other, and last night only proved that. No, she wasn't jealous over the Darcey thing, but taking it slow should help them navigate any more pitfalls.

Since her father died over a decade ago, she'd been alone, fending for herself, trying to keep his business going. There had been no time for fun or fooling around. Sure, she'd had boyfriends in high school and a couple of flings over the years, but nothing ever serious.

Besides, she knew she wasn't exactly the type guys went for. She was neither classically pretty or even feminine, had no fashion sense, her nails were always chipped, and her hair could be like a rat's nest most of the time. She also swore like a pirate, drank like a sailor, and had no brain-to-mouth filter. *Of course Cam would go for someone like Darcey.* Someone who was cute and girly and who'd learned how to put on makeup when she was a teenager instead of changing the oil in the engine of a 1951 Ford truck.

"I don't like that look on your face," he said, interrupting her thoughts. "What's the matter?"

"I ... it's fine." She waved a hand nonchalantly. "It's a long drive up; we should go."

They decided to drive up to Damon's cabin in his Range Rover since it would be more comfortable. He opened the door for her and helped her inside.

"Nice," she said as she eased into the front passenger seat, her hands feeling the buttery soft leather underneath her. "How'd you manage to snag this ride on your ranger salary?"

"Um, it's a rental," he said before closing the door. He walked around the front and slipped into the driver's seat.

"Damon's sent me the GPS coordinates, and I've programmed them in. Ready to leave?"

"As I'll ever be."

Cam started the engine, and they were off. Damon and Anna Victoria lived not too far from the rangers headquarters, in an area where Lennox Corporation, the company that owned the mountains, leased land to rangers. It was apparently one of the perks of the job, and Damon had a huge, beautiful two-story cabin on a large, secluded acreage.

"So, it's going to be a long drive," he began. "How about we get to know each other?"

"All right," she said. "What's your favorite color?"

He thought for a moment. "Green."

"Mine too. Looks like we're going to get along, champ," she joked.

He flashed her a wry smile. "All right then. Favorite food."

"Pizza. You?"

"Bangers and mash."

"A what now?"

"It's a British dish," he said. "It's basically sausages and mashed potatoes."

"Whew! I thought it was some kind of kinky thing ... not that I would mind." She winked at him.

They continued their game as the drive went on. She enjoyed learning all the little things his preferences revealed about him. And she was loving every minute of it, at least, she was until the last question.

"Favorite time of the year," he asked.

"Duh. Easy. Christmas."

"I meant season."

"Yeah, that's what I said. The Christmas season."

He frowned, but said nothing.

Sensing something was wrong, she turned to him. "What? What's wrong with Christmas?"

"Nothing."

The atmosphere inside the car definitely changed, growing darker. "You ... don't like Christmas?"

He flinched. "Not really."

"What? *Pffft*. I don't believe it. Everyone likes Christmas."

"That's an absolute statement, and therefore cannot be true." His eyes remained fixed on the road. "There are people out there who don't like Christmas."

"Yeah, heartless ogres!" *Oh my God, this couldn't be happening!* "You're a polar bear, how can you not like Christmas?"

"And what does that have to do with it?"

"Duh, you're Santa's neighbor. And didn't you ever see those Christmas commercials with the ice-skating polar bears?"

He pushed his glasses up the bridge of his nose. "You do know Santa Claus isn't real, right?"

The condescension in his tone rankled her. "That's not the point." This was slowly turning into her worst nightmare. "Stop the car."

"I beg your pardon?"

"Stop the car, I'm getting out."

He glanced at her, his face incredulous. "Out? And where do you think you're going?"

"Home."

"J.D., be reasonable. We're in the middle of the

mountains. It will take you hours before you can get back down on foot. You're not serious, are you?"

"You're not serious about hating Christmas, are you?" she shot back.

"For God's sake, stop being dramatic. Why does it matter if I do or don't?" His jaw hardened and those blue-violet eyes turned flinty. "Can we talk about something else?"

"Fine."

She wanted to press on and ask him why he had a heart a few sizes too small, but the tone of his voice and his sudden chilly demeanor made her think twice. Instead, she sank back into her seat and sulked. Her cat grumbled at her, irritated because she made their mate angry. *Well, it's not my fault he's a Scrooge.*

Thankfully they were already near Damon's house and the car ride didn't last any longer. As soon as Cam pulled up to the front of the cabin, she bolted out of the Range Rover and marched toward the door without looking back.

"Happy Thanksgiving—hey!" Gabriel protested when he opened the door and she dashed inside. "What crawled up your ass?"

Not minding Gabriel or greeting Damon, who was sitting on the huge sectional couch in the living room, she went straight toward the kitchen. As she guessed, Anna Victoria and Temperance were already there, placing boxes of Chinese takeout on the kitchen table. There was also fresh pie in the oven—pumpkin and apple, guessing by the smell.

"Hey, J.D. Happy Thanksgiving!" Temperance greeted, her pretty face lighting up, but then dimmed when her gaze landed on J.D.'s face. "What's the matter?"

"It ..." Oh God, how was she going to say this?

"J.D.?" Anna Victoria walked over to her. "Are you okay? What happened?"

Grabbing one of the kitchen stools, she hopped up onto it, then planted her chin in her hands. "It's a tragedy, ladies. A great big tragedy."

"Tragedy?" Temperance echoed.

"It's Cam ..." She paused. "He ... he ..."

"He what?" Anna Victoria asked. "Is it bad? Does he have a girlfriend?"

"Or a secret family stashed back in England?" Temperance offered.

She shook her head. "No, no. Even worse. He *hates* Christmas."

"Hates Christmas?" Anna Victoria frowned. "What do you mean? Who could hate Christmas?"

"Exactly." And she proceeded to tell them what happened during the ride over. "And then he went all cold on me. Like, he just shut down." And if she were honest with herself, that probably annoyed her the most. "I don't think this is going to work out."

The two women looked at each other. "Surely it's not that serious," Anna Victoria said. "You're mates, you should be able to work it out."

"But it's *Christmas*."

"Gabriel told me how this season means a lot to you," Temperance said. "And why."

"So did Damon." Anna Victoria nodded. "And I understand, believe me."

A lump began to form in J.D.'s throat. She didn't mind that her best friends told their mates, it wasn't like it was a secret. "Then you know why it's so important to me."

"*He* doesn't," Temperance pointed out.

She swallowed the lump, and her throat loosened enough to allow her to speak again. "I didn't have time to tell him. But I didn't think he'd be so against the holiday. What if he hates it so much that he won't ever want to celebrate it? Do you think he's maybe part of one of those weird cults that don't observe any kind of special holidays? What about birthdays and—"

"Slow down, J.D.," Anna Victoria chuckled. "I'm pretty sure he's not part of any cult. But"—she reached out and put a hand on her shoulder—"being mates, or any relationship for that matter, involves compromise."

"And communication," Temperance added.

"You guys just met yesterday, cut yourself some slack," Anna Victoria said. "And you know, I'm so proud of you guys, being so mature and taking things slow and wanting to get to know each other. This is part of that. And arguing and fighting and pushing each other's buttons."

"But in the end, it's all worth it, right, Anna Victoria?" Temperance said with a wink.

"Definitely."

The two shared a look again, but this time, both had that glow of happiness she'd only seen when they were talking about their mates. A pang of envy hit her—she wanted to someday have that look on her face too.

She gave a resigned sigh. And though her pride would take a hit, she knew she had been unreasonable for throwing a tantrum and blowing things out of proportion. "Comprise. Communication. Okay. Excuse me, ladies." Rolling up her sleeves, she marched back out to the living room.

The three men were already sitting on the couch,

drinking beers and watching football on the huge flatscreen TV. *Typical*, she thought. She marched over to Cam, who was right on the edge of the sectional, a beer in one hand. He looked up at her as she stood over him, face inscrutable. Though they kept their heads turned to the screen, Damon and Gabriel's gazes flickered to them.

"Is this seat taken?" she asked.

"Go ahead," he gestured to the empty spot next to him.

Instead of sitting next to him, she planted herself on top of his knees.

"That's my lap."

She crossed her arms over her chest. "Did I stutter, Spenser?"

Damon sighed and got up. "Let's go check on what the girls are doing, Gabriel."

The lion shifter rolled his eyes. "Right.

As soon as the two men left, Cam opened his mouth. "J.D.—"

"Wait." She held a hand up. "Let me go first. So, I may have overreacted a little about the whole Christmas thing. And I'm sorry for being overdramatic."

He looked at her, surprised. "I didn't think you would apologize."

"Yeah, well." She let out a huff. "It seems to me there was a lack of communication between us." Her shoulders sank. "Now, I'm not telling you this because I want you to feel sorry for me, okay? All I want is for you to understand. Why Christmas means so much to me, I mean." She sucked in a deep, calming breath. "My mom, she loved the holidays. Like, *a lot.*"

Her chest tightened. It had been so long ago, and if it

weren't for the pictures she had around the house or the home videos her father had kept, she wasn't sure if she would even remember the details of Ivy McNamara's face or the sound of her voice. "When Christmas rolled around, she would go all out, decorating our tiny Brooklyn apartment. One year, the tree she got was so big that Pop couldn't get it up our sixth-floor walkup. Had to rig a pulley to bring it up through our window. But he did it because he loved her so much and would do anything for her."

Cam's expression softened, and he cupped the side of her face. "When ... how ..."

She gave his palm a nuzzle and breathed in his scent. "Brain aneurism. She was human, and it was all very quick, and she felt no pain. I was nine." A tear rolled down her cheek, and he brushed it away. "I can still remember the l-last Christmas we spent together." The smell of fresh-baked cookies. Ribbons and wrapping paper everywhere. Ma and Pop kissing under the mistletoe. "The summer after she ... she ... we moved here to Blackstone so my father could open the garage and we could start afresh. New York was just ... everything back there reminded us of her. But when Christmas rolled around, we realized we couldn't let her down. We couldn't forget her, not during this time of the year."

"Bloody hell," Cam cursed, then pulled her in for a hug. "I'm sorry, love," he murmured into her hair. "So sorry."

She sniffed and wiped her eyes on his shoulder. "It's silly—"

"It's not," he said.

"It is. I'm a grown woman. They've both been gone for so long and I just ... it's a big deal to me, okay?"

"And now I know why." Hauling her around, he made her legs straddle him, then tilted her chin up. "I apologize for being harsh." His lips swept over hers gently. "And thank you for telling me."

She looked deep into his eyes, her thumb brushing a lock of hair that had loosened from his ponytail and clung to his cheek. The blue-violet orbs stared back, and she waited for him to say ... something. To give his own confession on why he hated Christmas. But they remained like that for a few heartbeats with neither speaking. *Maybe he just doesn't like the holidays. Weirdo.* But he was *her* weirdo. "So, I guess we just passed a milestone."

"Milestone?"

"Yeah. Our first fight."

"Hmm." He blinked. "I do believe you're right."

"Now it's time for another milestone—first kiss and make up." Moving her hips against his, she leaned down to press her lips to his. She must have caught him by surprise because he didn't move, but then quickly responded. *There ya go.*

A growl rattled from his chest as his hands moved down to cup her ass, pulling her closer against the growing tent in his pants. She shuddered when the ridge of his erection rubbed against her just right, and his tongue invaded her mouth to deepen their kiss. A hand reached up under her sweater, inching up her rib cage to cup her breast.

"*Ahem.*"

Cam's hands dropped to his sides as J.D. pulled away, glaring up at Damon, who stood at the doorway, arms crossed over his chest. "Do you mind?"

"As a matter of fact, I do," Damon grumbled. "You guys

already desecrated my office desk, and now you wanna do it to my sofa too?"

"Sorry, Chief." Cam eased her off his lap. "Won't happen again. I really promise this time."

"See that it doesn't. Now, let's go eat before the food gets cold," Damon cocked his head back toward the kitchen.

"Of course. Be with you in a moment," he called after the chief as he left. "That was close," he sighed.

"Not close enough." She smirked at him. He looked so cute, with his glasses askew and that flustered look on his face. "C'mon, champ. Let's go get some food."

Chapter 5

Chinese takeaway didn't seem like the typical Thanksgiving meal, but J.D., Damon, and Gabriel had explained their little tradition as they stood around the huge kitchen island filling up their plates from the numerous boxes.

"Since we moved to Blackstone, Pop and I always spent Thanksgiving with the Coopers," J.D. began. "He and I, well, neither of us were great cooks, so Damon's mom was only too happy to have us come over every year."

"She's an amazing cook," Gabriel said. "I mean, don't get me wrong, we had the best chefs prepare our Thanksgiving at my house, but it was always so formal and stuffy." His nose wrinkled. "I would always sneak out and come over to Damon's as soon as I could. We kept the tradition, even while Damon was deployed and when he came back."

"But my parents retired four years ago, sold their house, and moved to Florida," Damon continued. "I can't stand traveling during the holidays and even then, they prefer to come back to Blackstone for Christmas since they miss the snow."

"That first year, we tried to make Thanksgiving dinner, just the three of us at my house," J.D. said. "Unfortunately, it was a disaster."

"A total disaster," Gabriel added.

"You can still see the scorch marks on my ceiling." J.D. slapped her palm over her eyes. "The only restaurant open was Chang Kee, and so we had to order there, and we've been doing that ever since."

They got their fill of food, and the rest of the day was spent drinking beers and watching American football on the telly with each couple finding their own spot on the humungous couch in the living room. He and J.D. were at the far end of the section with her tucked into his side.

He smiled against her hair, and his bear rumbled happily. Earlier, of course, it had been a complete beast. It hated that he had angered their mate and made her storm off. But she was being completely unreasonable during that fight in the car, wanting to get out in the middle of the road just because he didn't like Christmas. Of course, he felt terrible and wanted to kick himself when she had confessed to him about her mother. He understood her obsession with the holiday now and how much it meant to her.

The only problem was, he didn't just dislike Christmas.

He *abhorred* it.

Each year, he did his best to avoid the holidays. He buried himself in research and work, ensuring he was away doing fieldwork as far away as he could possibly manage in places where they didn't celebrate the holidays.

Each year that December twenty-fifth passed, he could breathe a sigh of relief.

It was too much to bear.

Too many memories.

Too much baggage.

Now, however, as he held his mate to his side, he knew that he would have to find a way to make it through the holiday, because he found himself wanting to make her happy. He would do anything to be with her, and so he would grin and bear it. Adapt that stiff upper lip his father's people were known for.

Besides, Christmas was only one day of the year, and there was still a month to go before the actual holiday. How bad could it be?

"Oh dear, am I reading that clock right?" Anna Victoria said with yawn. "It's nearly midnight."

After an afternoon of watching football, they had gone back and reheated more of the Chinese food for a late supper. Then Damon started a fire in the fireplace, and they all gathered around, drinking and chatting. Cam for the most part, was content to have J.D. snuggling in his arms, listening to the three friends reminisce about their childhood.

Temperance raised her head from where it was lying on Gabriel's chest. "Oh wow, I didn't realize it was that late."

Cam cleared his throat. "I guess we should be going."

"Oh, hells yeah!" J.D. bounded up and raised a fist in the air. "Thanksgiving is almost over. Woot, woot!"

"You're awfully happy to be having this day over," Anna Victoria said with a chuckle. "I thought you liked Thanksgiving."

"I do. But having Thanksgiving over means one thing."

"Oh no," Gabriel groaned. "Please God, no."

"What's the matter?" Temperance asked.

"Is it Black Friday?" Anna Victoria supplied.

Damon shook his head. "No, it's—"

J.D. reached for the hem of her top and whipped it off. "Yeah baby!" Underneath her Thanksgiving jumper was another one—this time, it was Christmas themed and had a picture of a candy cane with two, well-positioned holly berries at the base. The text underneath read, *Well Hung.* "Merry Christmas!"

"That," Damon finished with a shake of his head.

Dear God, not again, Cam thought.

"Yes, and you know what that means." J.D.'s eyes twinkled. "Damon, is your axe in the shed?"

"Axe?" Cam said incredulously. "What do you need an axe for?"

"It's time for my favorite tradition that marks the beginning of the season. We're going to go get my Christmas tree!"

Cam frowned. "But surely there aren't any tree farms open at this time."

"Tree farm? *Pffft.*" She waved him away. "Who needs a farm when we have an entire mountain full of trees?"

"But that's illegal. The Lennoxes own the mountains, and they forbid the cutting down of trees. It's one of the very first things I read in the ranger handbook." He looked to Damon. "Right? For example, you might technically own this house, but the land it's sitting on is on a ninety-nine year lease, owned by Lennox. J.D., love, you could get in trouble if you try and chop down a tree." Not to mention, the Lennoxes, were a family of dragons who would not take kindly to having their land defaced.

"That's correct." The corner of Damon's mouth tugged up. "But you're looking at the only person in the entire Blackstone town, possibly the world, who has special permission to cut down any tree in the mountains for her Christmas tree."

"He means me," J.D. said smugly.

"You? How?"

"Well," J.D. began, cocking her hip, "back in senior year of high school, I was at this party, right? You know the story, some kid's parents were away for the weekend, so they throw a party and there was stuff going on ..."

"Stuff?" Cam asked, brows furrowing together. "What kind of stuff?"

"Booze. Boys. Going upstairs. You know, stuff teens do when their parents aren't around."

His polar bear didn't like the sound of that. "And did you do some of this stuff?" He turned to Damon and Gabriel. "Where were you? Did you watch out for her?"

She rolled her eyes. "That's not the point of the story. Anyway, I show up late, and this house was like wall-to-wall with kids from school. Including Sybil Lennox. Ever hear of her?"

If she only knew. "You said there were lots of people there from your high school."

"Yeah, well Sybil wasn't even in high school then, I think. She had to be what, thirteen? Somehow, she wound up there and got stinking drunk. Like, I knew the alcohol would wear off quickly, but she just kept taking shot after shot like liquor was going out of style. None of her usual friends were there, so she was hanging out with these older girls. Anyway, I'm not sure what happened, but one thing led to another, and someone pushes her in the pool. All these kids started cheering. I think they were waiting for her to shift into her dragon form or something, but she doesn't come up, so I jump in and fish her out."

Anna Victoria gasped. "Oh Lord, was she okay?"

"Yeah. She was just disoriented, and she sobered up pretty quick. But she wasn't feeling great, and so I offered to take her home. On the drive there, she told me that she had a huge blowup with her mom and dad. Something about her older brother, Luke. That's why she was so upset and snuck into the party. Anyway, I'm pulling up to the front of the castle and guess who's waiting there by the door? Her dad, the Blackstone Dragon himself. They make up and everything, and Sybil tells her dad what I did. So, Mr. Lennox is, like, super grateful, and he said I could have anything I wanted as a reward for helping his only daughter. And so yadda, yadda, yadda, Hank Lennox gives me permission to chop down any tree I want from the mountains every Christmas. In perpetuity."

Cam gaped at her. "So, what you're telling me is that a powerful billionaire dragon Alpha offered you *anything* for saving his daughter, and you ask to kill a tree from his property every year for the rest of your life?"

"If it makes you feel any better, that was my second choice."

"Dare we ask what the first one was?"

"I asked if he could set Jenny Blake's hair on fire as revenge for calling me a grease monkey," she replied. "But he wasn't too crazy about doing that."

The absurdity of it all made his head throb. But this was his J.D. they were talking about.

"So," she turned to Damon and Gabriel. "Are we going or what? I think I'd like a spruce or Douglas fir this year."

"Aw, do we have to?" Gabriel grumbled. "It's midnight and it's dark outside. Plus, there's trees and dirt and shit and ..."

"Aw, what else is wrong, Russel? Does your vagina hurt?" With an exasperated breath, she turned to Damon. "Well?"

Damon looked at her sheepishly. "I was kind of hoping we could at least wait until tomorrow? Why don't you stay over tonight, and we'll go at first light. I don't want to leave Anna Victoria alone tonight. At least she can join us in the morning."

"Damon, it's all right," his mate said. "I'll be fine. You should go."

"It's my bear. You know what it's like, especially now in your condition. It doesn't want to leave you behind."

"Oh c'mon. Really? You guys suck!" J.D. pouted. "This is tradition."

"I'll go with you," Cam offered.

She whirled around. "You will?"

"Of course." As if he was going to let her traipse around the woods alone in the dark. Besides, it was one chance to finally be alone with her. "I'm your mate." His bear wholeheartedly agreed.

"Yay!" She leaned down and kissed him on the cheek. "Let me go get the axe, and I'll meet you outside!"

As soon as J.D. was out of earshot, Gabriel turned to him. "Ooh boy. Good luck with that."

"Good luck?" He stood up and brushed some lint off his

jeans. "We're just going out to chop down a tree. How hard could it be?"

Gabriel and Damon looked at each other, then burst out laughing.

Cam frowned. *This does not bode well.*

Cam felt like they'd been outside for hours, though his watch said it had only been fifty-five minutes since they had left the cabin. *No wonder those two laughed at me like hyenas.*

He and J.D. started walking into the woods behind Damon's home. The damn place was teeming with pine trees, yet J.D. refused to stop until they found "the perfect one."

"How about that one?" Cam asked, pointing to a five-foot-tall spruce. "That's a good one."

J.D. wrinkled her nose. "Too short."

He glanced around and nodded at a six-foot scotch pine.

"Too stubby. C'mon, champ," she waved at him to keep following her. "The best ones are deeper in the forest."

Grumbling to himself, he trudged after her. He made a few more suggestions, but she vetoed all of them. They were "too tall" or "not tall enough" or "too crooked" or "too bushy."

"This one." He grabbed the branch of a white pine. "This one's perfect."

Her eyes narrowed at his selection, and she tapped a finger on her chin as she contemplated on it. "*Hmmm.*"

"What does *hmmm* mean?" he asked, impatient.

"It is the right height. And the right bushiness. But it's too ... piney."

"Too *piney?*" he exclaimed, throwing the axe on the

ground. "It's a pine tree. They're all bloody pine trees! Of course they're going to be piney! What else would they be?"

"Jesus, Cam, I can practically see the steam coming out of your ears." She laughed out loud. "You look like you're going to have a heart attack."

"Confound it, woman, you're going to give me one if you don't choose a damn tree!"

She sighed and walked over to him, then reached up to touch the side of his face. "Please Cam, it has to be perfect. This is a special tree."

"Special?"

"Yeah. It's our first tree together."

"Our tree?" He blinked.

"Yeah, I mean ... first one we're getting as mates." Her lips curled up into a smile. "If you'll just be a little more patient with me, I'll give you something you want."

Now she was talking. "Oh really? What would that be?"

"Well ... how about I show you my animal?"

His bear very much liked that idea. And frankly, so did he. It felt like a step in the right direction. "All right. But I want payment first."

"Payment?"

He crossed his arms over his chest. "You heard me. I've been mucking about the woods looking for your tree for an hour. I want to see it. Your animal. Time to pay the piper."

"Fine." She shoved the sleeves of her jumper up to her elbows. "Stand back."

Obeying, he took a step back. His polar bear stood up on its hind legs, excited. He, too, felt the crackle of electricity in the air as he waited with bated breath, his eyes never leaving hers.

Fur sprouted on her face as her long hair receded under her cap. He expected her limbs to stretch and grow, but to his surprise, they began to shrink instead. Moments later, she was gone, and only a heap of clothing and her trucker cap were left on the ground. "J.D.?" he called. His polar bear paced, feeling uneasy that their mate was gone.

Something moved from under the pile of clothing. Bending down, he pulled the cap away. "J.D.?"

Two hazel blinked up at him, gray specks twinkling in the moonlight. A small feline padded out from the neckline of J.D.'s Christmas jumper, revealing more of itself. It had vertical horizontal stripes along its neck, front paws, and tail, but spots all around its body. *"Felis nigripes,"* he whispered. "The African black-footed cat. Hello," he greeted, giving it a scratch on the head. "Oh!"

The little creature—measuring less than fifteen inches tall—crawled up his arm, then rubbed its little head against his chin. "There, there ... aren't you a pretty thing." He stroked its soft fur. "What a beautiful creature you are," he whispered. He loved that she was one of the rarest cats in the world. Hell's bells, he didn't even know there were shifters of her kind. It made him feel special, knowing she was his mate, and she trusted him enough to show her.

His bear, too, glowed with happiness. He could practically feel it begging to be let out. J.D.'s cat let out a mewl. "You can feel my bear," he stated. "It wants to meet you too."

The cat purred.

"All right then." He set the cat down gently, then took two steps back, and began to undress. The initial touch of the chilly air made gooseflesh rise on his skin, but his body quickly adjusted. And then he let his animal out.

They must have looked quite a sight, a humongous ten-foot polar bear and the tiny feline. The bear lay down, then went still, waiting for the cat to approach. After a few wary blinks, J.D.'s cat padded over and gave the bear a few sniffs. Eventually, it purred and rubbed its body around the bear's side.

To Cam's surprise, the tiny creature climbed up its flank, sharp claws digging in with pleasure as it meowed. The bear stiffened and bore the pain, allowing the cat to explore its back. Eventually it reached the bear's head, then crawled down to the ground, stopping in front of him. Turning its face around, it gave a 'come hither' look, then darted into the trees.

The bear chased after their mate. With their excellent shifter senses, they were able to catch up, though Cam had no doubt in his mind that if J.D. wanted to, she and her cat could have easily evaded them.

The cat zoomed up a tree, but not far enough that the polar bear couldn't reach it. It swiped its mighty paws up, trying to coax the cat to come down. Eventually, the feline relented and climbed down the polar bear's arm and body, then jumped and landed on its feet.

The bear was about to lumber around to face the feline, but to Cam's surprise, a pair of slim, fully human arms wrapped around his bear's torso.

"You know what I am," J.D. said as she rubbed her cheek on his fur.

I need her, Cam told his bear. *Please*.

The polar bear hesitated but released its hold on their body.

Soon, he, too, was fully human. Turning around, he pressed her close. "Of course," he murmured against her silken hair. "It's my job. I study animals." He pressed a kiss to her temple, then cupped her face to stare into those gray-flecked hazel eyes. "You're gorgeous. Both of you. Why would you hide it?"

Hesitation crossed her face. "I'm not ... it's not that I'm ashamed of it. But you know. People don't know, and they always think I'm just a cat."

"Just a cat?" he asked incredulously. "How could anyone call you just a cat? You're the deadliest feline in the world. Sixty percent success rate when hunting. That means you can hunt more prey in a night than most apex predators can in a month. That's—*mmmm!*"

Her arms came around his neck to pull him down for a kiss. "You're amazing," she moaned against his mouth. "I knew there was a reason we were mates."

She arched her body against his, and the sudden awareness that they were both naked hit him at full force. "J.D.," he groaned as his cock twitched when it rubbed against her stomach. "Will you let me touch you? Everywhere? Just for a bit." *Just a taste for now.*

"You don't even have to ask," she panted.

He captured her mouth again, tasting her sweetness, then released her lips so he could step back and look at her. Her skin glowed in the moonlight, her hair like a halo around her flushed, aroused face. His gaze traced down to the ink on her arm—delicate vines of ivy curling around her bicep—before moving to her breasts.

Oh, fuck me.

Her breasts weren't overly large, just right for her slim frame, but her nipples—they were large and perfectly round, the pink areolas stiff and puffy.

He couldn't help himself as he bent his head and took one in his mouth. Fingers dug into his hair, nails scraping down his scalp as his tongue lashed against her right nipple. He sucked in her breast, while his other hand teased the left. Her scent flooded his nose, and he remembered tasting her last night, wanting that again. Slowly, he trailed kisses down over her stomach, getting down to his knees.

"Cam," she said. "*Cam!*"

His inattention got him a yank on his scalp, which sent his desire deflating. *Among other things.* "What?" he asked in an annoyed tone, looking up at her.

"Look!" She pointed to something behind him.

"Is there someone here?" Turning his head, he focused his sight to detect any movement in the tree.

"No, silly," she said. "There. That's it."

"What's it?"

"My—our tree," she squealed, pulling away from him and then dashing toward a lone Colorado blue spruce about six feet behind them.

He groaned as he got to his feet, then trudged toward her. "Are you sure?" It looked like any other tree in the forest, but then again, he couldn't exactly focus on it, not when she was right beside it, fully naked, her gorgeous nipples on display as her breasts bounced deliciously when she jumped up and down in excitement.

"Yes, I'm sure." Her eyes lit up. "C'mon, let's get dressed and grab the axe."

They went back to where they first shifted, retrieved their clothes and the tree. Though he grumbled the entire time, it was worth it, seeing his mate so happy. And despite his feelings toward this holiday, he knew he could endure it, if it meant seeing her all aglow like this.

They dragged the tree back to the cabin, where they loaded it onto the back of Damon's truck. The chief had promised to deliver it first thing in the morning since there was no way they could safely bring it down in the Range Rover. When it was secure, they got into his vehicle and made their way back into town.

J.D. must have been exhausted, because she drifted off to sleep halfway through the drive. When they reached her home, he stopped outside her driveway, got out and went to her side to open the door for her. "J.D.?" He gently shook her awake.

Her eyes fluttered open. "What—oh!" She blinked and sat up. "Sorry," she yawned. "Must have fallen asleep. Are we back?"

"Yes."

"You should have woken me to keep you company."

"I didn't mind."

"Finally got some silence, huh?" she teased. "That's okay, I know I can be a bit ... loud."

A bit was an understatement. "I don't mind you being yourself." And he meant that. J.D. was like a force of nature, but one he couldn't turn away from. "Besides, you're beautiful when you sleep."

"Oh yeah? Wanna come in and watch me sleep some more?"

"Don't tempt me," he warned, though he kept his tone lighthearted. "Back there, I almost lost control."

"Would it be so bad?"

His bear agreed with her. But he still wasn't sure. "I thought we agreed—"

"I know. Get to know each other more." With a sigh, she slipped out of the seat. "And I guess it would be nice to have you on a real bed at some point."

"Agreed," he said. "Now, let me walk you to your door."

"Such a gentleman," she teased, but put her hand in his as they walked together. "So," she began. "How about you come over in the morning, and we can decorate our tree?"

"Sounds like a plan." Leaning down, he gave her a chaste kiss on the forehead. "Thank you for showing me your animal, love."

"My cat's crazy about you," she said. "And that's a big compliment, believe me. It can be a bitch when it wants to."

"And my bear adores you both." A happy rumble emanated from his chest, as if to prove his point. "I'll come by with breakfast."

"All right. Good night, Cam," she said as she unlocked her door. "I'll see you in the morning."

"Good night."

He waited until he heard the click of her lock before turning back and heading to his car, slipped in and drove back to his flat.

When he first came here, he had arranged to rent a fully furnished penthouse in the newer development of South Blackstone. He'd only glanced at the photos online and snapped up the first available one, not really caring what it looked like. When he moved in, he only had one suitcase and his backpack with his laptop and research.

The building was modern, which he appreciated, so everything was electronic and automatic, from the garage gates that picked up the RFID sensor on his Range Rover, to the sensors in the elevator and door lock that activated via his key fob. As soon as he got into his flat, he walked over to the plush sofa and sat down on it, heaving a long sigh.

If he really wanted to—and he did—he could run back and knock on J.D.'s door, and she'd welcome him into her bed. He'd practically begged her tonight and he almost gave in. Surely if he had tasted her again, he would have taken her right then and there. But still—

His phone ringing jolted him out of his thoughts, and he quickly fished it out of his pocket. When he saw the name on the caller ID, he let out another sigh. He contemplated ignoring it or sending it to voicemail, but that wouldn't stop her. So, he picked it up.

"Hello, *babushka*," he greeted his grandmother, his brain immediately switching to Russian. "How nice of you to call. What time is it over there?"

"Aleksandr." Natalia Dashokov preferred using his Russian middle name. His *real* name, as she would call it. "How are you, *lyuba*? Why have you not called me?" The tone in her voice was just the right amount of sweetness, pouting, and guilt-inducing reproach.

"Forgive me." He flinched inwardly. "I have been busy these past few days. There was a nest of rare red-tailed grouses that I'd been observing from the early hours of the day until evening, when the parents go out and hunt...." Cam was pretty sure there were no such thing as red-tailed grouses, but this was his usual distraction tactic whenever Natalia called. She would either get bored or impatient, but eventually forgive him.

"*Bah!*" she interrupted. "That is no excuse for ignoring your frail old grandmother."

Frail was not a word he would use to describe her. For a human, she could be even more tenacious and pugnacious than any shifter or animal. "Again, my apologies." He shifted the phone to his other ear. "And to what do I owe this call, *babushka?*"

"You *know* why I am calling."

His chest tightened, making it hard to speak.

"Your time in America is at an end. I want to know when you intend to fly back to London."

Had he forgotten his promise to her? And his obligations?

When he had seen her on New Year's Eve, he had begged Natalia for one just one more year of unfettered study before he took on his family "obligations." After completing his second PhD, the opportunity came up to study the flora and fauna of the famed Blackstone mountains. When he had moved out here, all he wanted to do was devote his time to his research for his last months of freedom. He had never expected to meet his mate, much less in America of all places.

And now, with J.D. involved in the mix, things were about to get more complicated.

Should he tell his grandmother about her? While that would send Natalia over the moon, it would make things even more difficult. He loved Natalia, but she meddled too much.

And then there was J.D., who knew absolutely nothing about his background and his promise to his grandmother. How would she react? Would she want to leave Blackstone and everything and everyone she knew to start a new life with him in a new country?

"*Lyuba?*" Natalia's voice broke his train of thought. "Thinking with that big brain of yours again?"

He swallowed. She was one of the few people who understood how his mind worked, who didn't mind if he was too absorbed in his own thoughts. "I ... I'm just finishing up some things here." This was not a conversation he should be having with her on the phone. "I ... there are a few things I need to take care of and then ... then we can speak. Perhaps in January, when I fly back?" Yes, that would give him some time to weigh his options and think on things.

"January?" she said incredulously. "But that is so far away. Next year, even. You told me last year when your final term began that all you needed was *one* year. And the year is almost over."

"I know, *babushka*, but you can't expect me to fly out right before midnight on December thirty-first. I'm not Cinderella, and I won't turn into a pumpkin." He sighed. "I promise ... I'll be back, all right? Don't you fret. And I may have good news for you too." *Like those great grandchildren you've always wanted.*

And that was one reason he couldn't tell her about J.D. yet. Natalia would probably fly out here and lock them in a room together until J.D. popped out a cub or two.

"Good news?" Now she sounded even more intrigued.

"Yes, *babushka*. It's a surprise. And don't you even try to guess," he warned. "I don't want to ruin it."

"Hmmm ... all right. But I want you to keep me abreast of your move back. Do not forget to call your dear grandmother, eh?"

"Yes, I promise."

"I shall speak *and* see you soon, *lyuba*," she said before hanging up.

Bloody hell.

Tossing his phone aside, he sank back into the cushions and massaged the pressure building between his eyebrows. He had been hoping his grandmother wouldn't take their one-year bargain so literally, but it seemed she was determined to have what she was owed. Or rather, delivery on what *she* owed.

Everything would have to progress much faster, now that the clock was ticking. *Goddammit.* He really wanted to get to know J.D. and ease her into things. And from what little he did know of her, it wasn't going to be an easy transition.

The life he had been prepared for—no, bred for—was light years away from what she knew. It might crush her spirit, the obligations and the rigidity of it all. And then there was the question if she would even want it. She had no idea what being his mate would be really about.

He needed some time to think. Some space away from her and figure out what to do next. This situation needed some analysis, and he needed time to figure out the pros and cons, and how exactly he was going to tell her the truth of who he was.

Chapter 6

"Thanks guys!" J.D. waved goodbye to Anna Victoria and Damon as they pulled out of her driveway. As promised, they delivered the Christmas tree that morning. "Have a great breakfast!"

"You too!" Anna Victoria shouted back, then winked. "And if I don't see you for yoga class tomorrow, I won't be surprised."

J.D. grinned as the truck drove off. *Oh yeah.* Last night had been so close. If she hadn't seen the perfect tree, she would have let Cam touch her everywhere for definitely more than "just a little bit." True, it had only been three days now since they had met, but for God's sake, how much slower could they go? If they counted the party and yesterday, then that would mean today would be their third date.

Even if we didn't go all the way, there were other things we could do, she thought. It sounded like Cam would be open to at least get to second or third base.

However, that would have to wait, as she already had the day planned. Put up the Christmas tree. Decorate it while drinking hot chocolate. And then cuddle on the couch with some of her favorite holiday movies. Then snuggling could lead to more. She licked her lips in anticipation.

Heading back inside her house, she walked over to the corner spot where her—or rather, her and Cam's—tree stood. The blue spruce was the perfect size and shape for the living room, and while the timing had been terrible when she spotted it, she just had to have it. The boxes of decorations taken out of storage now sat on her coffee table, and the hot chocolate made from scratch was ready. Now she only needed a sexy, brainy doctor to come knocking on her door, and everything would be perfect.

The familiar sound of her ringtone sent her scrambling for her phone. A thrill shot up her spine when she saw Cam's name on the caller ID. "Hey, Cam," she greeted, trying to sound casual. "Are you on the way? What breakfast didja get me?"

"Good morning, love." His voice made her all tingly, especially when he called her with that pet name. "I'm afraid I have some bad news."

"Oh? Did you have trouble finding restaurants that were open today?" Many businesses in Blackstone would be closed over the long weekend so people could spend time with their families. Cam, not being from around here, wouldn't have known that. "I should have realized and told you—"

"No, it's not that." He let out a breath. "Something's come up. I'm afraid I can't make it over."

"Can't make it over?" Disappointment coursed through her. "What's wrong? Are you all right? What happened?" Surely if Cam couldn't make it, there was something really wrong.

"I just ... I have to deal with something."

"What thing? Is it an emergency?"

"A ... family matter."

She waited for him to explain. For a second, she even thought the line went dead as the silence stretched on. "Cam?"

"Yes?"

"Is everything okay?"

"Yes."

Then why was he bailing out? She couldn't understand. But then again, surely she didn't imagine what happened yesterday and last night. *I should give him the benefit of the doubt.* Though she and Cam were mates, if something happened to Gabriel or Damon, she would drop everything in an instant to be with them. "All right." She plopped down on the couch. "If you change your mind ..."

"I'll let you know. Goodbye, J.D."

"Bye, Cam." And the line went dead.

Her cat dug its claws into her stomach, making her feel even more uneasy. *You're being silly*, she told herself. Besides she and Cam didn't really know each other. This was the time they were supposed to use to do that, and this was part of it. Also, a day or two away from each other would slow things down and let them figure out how they were going to do this.

Her animal, however, disagreed and sank its claws deeper into her, as if telling her that something was wrong.

"Silly cat," she said, brushing her inner animal's protest away. Getting up from the couch, she decided to drink her hot chocolate for breakfast and then see what movies were on the television. She looked at the boxes of decorations sadly, but maybe Cam would finish early with his family emergency and they could still make something of today.

The rest of the day passed and there was no call or even text from Cam. And J.D. was sure she didn't miss any because she constantly glanced at her phone. Every notification made her jump, but none of them were from him. She ordered pizza for lunch, had leftovers for dinner, and then went to bed. *He'll call tomorrow*, she told herself.

But Cam didn't call the next day or the day after that. The diner had opened on Sunday, at least, so she was able to get out of the house and go somewhere for a meal instead of eating day-old pizza and Chinese food again. She didn't want to call any of her friends to hang out because they were all busy, and inevitably, they would ask her where Cam was. She couldn't bear to tell them that she didn't know. When she got home, the sight of the bare tree and the decorations in their boxes made her stomach clench. Her cat sniffed and flicked its short tail in a motion that she read as *I told you so*.

By the time she went into the garage the next day, her disappointment had turned to irritation. Contrary to what most people thought, if J.D. was having an off day, she was never irrationally angry at her employees. No, Pop would never have stood for anyone taking out their frustration on loyal people. She really only got mad when they did shoddy work or treated customers badly.

However, everyone in the garage knew to never cross her, and today, it was as if they could sense the simmering anger bubbling inside her, and they steered clear. For most of the morning and the rest of the day, she was quiet and sullen, giving them only one-word answers and mumbles when they asked her anything.

The afternoon rolled around, and there was not even a peep from Cam. Well, now J.D. was furious. Her cat spurred her on, vexed at her for not seeking their mate out earlier and very much pissed at him for not coming to see them.

It wasn't even quitting time when, in a fit of indignation, she grabbed her keys and left the garage. As she drove up to the Blackstone Rangers headquarters, that simmering anger had slowly turned into full-blown rage.

She arrived at HQ, fit to be tied, bursting through the doors. "Where can I find Dr. Spenser?" she asked the ranger guarding the front desk.

The young man looked up at her, eyeing her warily, probably sensing her and her animal's mood. "Uh, maybe I can help you, ma'am?"

"You can help by telling me where Dr. Spenser is."

He swallowed, his Adam's apple bobbing up and down nervously. "Who?"

"Cam. Spenser." She slammed her palm on the desk, emphasizing each word. "You know. Tall, blond, broody polar bear? Wears gold-rimmed glasses?"

"I—"

"Hey, J.D., how's it going?"

Whirling her head, she saw Daniel Rogers coming up to them. "Daniel, thank God you're here."

"Yeah? What's up?" He lifted his chin at the other ranger. "Hey, Dune, how's it going?"

Dune's eyes widened. "Um, hey, Daniel. Maybe you can help out Miss ... Miss ... uh ..."

"It's McNamara," she snapped.

"M-Miss McNamara is looking for someone."

"Oh yeah? Who?" Daniel asked.

She gritted her teeth. "Cam."

"Cam?" His brows drew together.

"Yeah, Cam. Do you know where he is?"

"Sure. At this time, he's probably in his office. Second floor—hey, wait!"

But she didn't bother to let him finish, and instead, stomped toward the elevators to take her to the second floor. Of course, she realized she should have asked Daniel which room, but it only took her three tries before finding the correct one.

"Cam Spenser, where the hell are you?" she announced as she burst through the third door.

Someone shot up from where they had their head down on a desk piled with papers and envelopes. "What the—" Cam stopped, rubbed his eyes, and grabbed his glasses to put them on. "J-J.D.?" He blinked. "What are you doing here?"

She clenched her jaw. "What am I doing here? What am *I* doing here?"

He harrumphed. "You don't have to repeat it to me, I asked you the question."

"I thought you said you had a family emergency."

"I said I had to deal with a family matter," he pointed out. "It was you who concluded it was an emergency."

Was he for real? "Seriously? You're playing semantics with me right now?"

Getting up to his feet, he combed his fingers through his loose hair, then tugged down at his rumpled shirt. "I don't understand why you're in a snit. I told you I had to deal with something and that I would call you once it was all sorted out." He rubbed a hand across his jaw, which was normally clean-shaven but now sported a stubble.

"But why are you here?" she asked.

"Why not?" he shrugged. "Work helps me think. And I wasn't really planning on having any days off after Thanksgiving, so I thought I'd drive back here and do some cleaning up and work so I can start afresh on Monday."

"Start afresh on ... Cam, it's Monday."

He blinked. "Excuse me?"

"It's. Monday. Today," she fumed. "You haven't called me in days." The way her voice trembled uncontrollably and her heart twinged made her even more furious. The only man who ever made her cry was her father, and that was because he had left her when he died.

He stared at her, mouth gaping open. "I ... I didn't mean to. But this ... this is how I am, I'm afraid. My work sometimes consumes me, and I don't always know which way is up. There was this time I was in the bogs of Stirling,..."

She waited for him to explain further. To tell her what his family emergency—matter—was and to ask for her forgiveness. But he only went on and on about bogs and fens and other shit she didn't know or care about. "Cam!"

"I—yes?"

"What's the real deal here?"

"Real ... deal?"

Oh, he tried to sound innocent. He probably droned on and on about mires and moss to distract her. But, looking into those blue-violet eyes, she could tell he was hiding something. "Yes. What's really going on? If you didn't want to decorate our—the tree with me, then you should have just said so."

"You and that damned tree," he grumbled. "And bloody fucking Christmas."

A pain slashed at her chest, and her cat reached out wanting to swipe at him. "You ... Scrooge!"

"Why is it always about this damned season? I can't fucking wait for it to be over and—wait." Panic struck his face. "That's not what I—"

"You know why this means so much to me!"

"J.D., please!" He rounded the table. "Please, I didn't mean that ... I'm just so goddamned exhausted ... I know your mum ..."

"Don't!" she hissed. "Don't you dare even think about her!" Motherfucker, she was going to lose her shit if she didn't get out of here. Spinning on her heel, she raced out of the office and down the hallway, heading toward the stairs instead of waiting for the elevator.

If he did call her or chase after her, she didn't know, and she didn't care. She raced to her truck like fucking Satan was on her heels, then peeled out of the parking lot as fast as she could.

Her body felt numb throughout the entire drive home, her mind refusing to accept what had happened. If he needed a few days to figure things out or if he just didn't want to decorate with her, she would have understood. But he fucking lied to her and that, she couldn't forgive. Her cat, too, seethed with displeasure.

Her phone was blowing up the entire drive down, but she ignored it. But it kept ringing and ringing, and so as soon as she got off the mountain roads and stopped at a light, she picked it up. "Get bent, Spenser!" she screamed, then tossed the phone at the passenger seat. "Asshole." It was immature, but it sure made her feel a helluva whole lot better.

When she reached home, she swerved into her driveway

and slammed on the brakes. As she was about to grab the door handle, her phone started ringing again. *Damn it.* Gritting her teeth, she picked it up. "In case we're having a cross-cultural miscommunication here, get bent means fuck off!"

"J-J.D.?"

Crap. It wasn't Cam. "Uh, who is this?"

"It's me. Roy."

Fucking Roy Jorrell. Just what she needed now. Her inner cat spat and swiped its claws out. "Sorry. Prank callers. What's up?"

"I was just ... you know. Checking in on you. You didn't answer my text the other day, but then I thought you're probably busy with the holiday weekend."

"Yeah, I was," she snapped impatiently. "Was there something you needed?"

"Me? Nah. I stopped by your garage, and they said you left earlier than usual."

"And?" She rolled her eyes. "Listen, I can't really talk right now. If you need stuff taken care of with your truck, just drop it by the garage, okay?"

"No, I was wondering if you had a chance to think—"

"Bye, Roy." She tossed the phone back into the passenger seat. Ugh, she didn't want to talk to him. Or anyone right now.

As she stomped into her living room, she considered tossing out that fucking tree and returning the decorations back into the attic.

However, when her gaze landed on the picture above her mantle, her stomach twisted. It was of her, Pop, and Mom when she was about four years old, on Christmas morning, of course. They were sitting in front of a tree, a pile of toys and scattered gift-wrapping paper around them.

"I'm sorry, Ma," she sniffed. "I would never throw out a perfectly good Christmas tree." And yes, it was *her* tree. "Don't worry, I'll make her pretty, just like you would have wanted."

With a determined grunt, she reached for the first box and opened it up. Mate or not, she would feel the fucking Christmas spirit this year, even if it killed her.

Chapter 7

If she was disappointed that Cam hadn't tried to contact her since their blow up, J.D. didn't show it. She just went about her life over the last few days as she always did. With the holidays in full swing and the weather starting to get colder, it was as busy as ever in the garage.

Her cat, however, turned into a moody little bitch. More than usual, anyway. Its emotions swung from anger at Cam for lying to them, and dejection at the fact that he had stayed away all this time.

But we don't want to see him, she told her animal.

It planted its chin on its front paws and pouted at her.

"Ugh."

Ignoring her cat, she continued on with her work. She had a bunch of cars that needed oil, antifreeze, and tire changes, not to mention heating system repairs and cleaning. Normally, she would leave basic stuff like this to her guys, but they were backed up. Besides, it was good to keep her hands busy, and frankly, she loved the work. It gave her a sense of purpose and reminded her a lot of growing up here, learning from and eventually working with her father.

When she finished the last car for the day, she went around, checking if her guys needed anything. Her last stop was on the east end of the compound which was separate from the car repair area. Entering the covered garage, she greeted the lone occupant inside. "Hey, Mason, what's up?"

The tall, burly bearded man looked up from where he was working on a dirt bike. "J.D," Mason Grimes greeted. "What's up? How was your Thanksgiving?"

Mason was her partner in the motorcycle shop she had on-site. Aside from doing repair work, he also did his custom bikes here. She counted herself lucky that Mason came along at the right time last year, as she nearly lost her investment when her previous partner had pulled out. Now, they were making money hand over fist as she could accept repairs from Blackstone residents rather than sending them to the next shop over in Verona Mills.

"You know, same old, same old." She ignored her cat's meowing protests. "How about you? How are the little ones?"

"They're great." His eyes always lit up when anyone mentioned his kids. "Tomorrow's the start of the Christmas Carnival at Lennox Park. Cassie's pretty excited to go. Amelia might stay home with James if it gets too nippy."

She chuckled. "Awesome, I'm sure she'll love it." Mason's little girl Cassie was hilarious, and J.D. loved the spunky four-year-old.

"And you? You're heading over, right? I know you never miss the first night when they turn on all the lights."

"Maybe." *Stupid Cam*, she thought. Frankly, she'd thrown herself into work so much that she'd forgotten, and for probably the first time in, well, ever, she wasn't feeling the Christmas spirit. "I got a lot to take care of. You know, the usual holiday rush. Anyway, just wanted to catch up with you on a few things."

They chatted for a few minutes about work, then J.D. bid him goodbye. As she headed back to the office, she saw one of her guys, Junior, coming out of the trailer. "Were you looking for me?"

Junior nodded. "You got a delivery, boss. Placed it on your desk."

"Delivery? I'm not expecting anything? What is it?"

A smile tugged up his mouth. "You'll see." The smile turned into a grin and then scampered away, as if he was trying to hide some juicy secret.

Shrugging, she pushed the door to the trailer open. "What the—" To her surprise, a large teddy bear sat on her desk. "Where the hell ..."

Cam.

Her heart soared, and she giggled like an idiot as she closed the door behind her, looking around as if someone might catch her doing something bad. Dashing over to the table, she took the white card clutched between the bear's paws. *Thinking of you, my mate.* It was printed out and not signed, but who else could it be from?

Her cat, however, let out a *mee-reow* and wrinkled its delicate little nose, like it smelled something distasteful, then flicked its tail.

"Oh, who asked you?" She held the card to her chest. *Oh, Cam ...*

Despite the excitement bubbling up in her, she knew a cute gift wasn't enough to make up for what he did. It was a nice thought, but she needed an explanation. Checking her phone, she frowned as her notifications tab sat empty. No missed calls, no text messages. *Hmmm.*

Cam didn't call that day or the next day. However, another delivery came. This time it was a huge—no, gigantic—arrangement of flowers. She took a whiff of the red and white roses—two dozen of them, each the size of a child's fist, arranged beautifully with other decorative leaves in a beautiful crystal vase. Plucking the card sticking out from the top, she opened it and read it aloud.

"You're my dream come true, my one and only mate."

Huh.

Not that she didn't like the sentiment behind it, but it just didn't sound like Cam. Plus, once again, the note wasn't signed.

A knock on the door made her jump. "Come in!" she said automatically without realizing whoever it was would see the flowers. Of course, Junior would probably have spread the word around about the boss getting gifts two days in a row now, and they were going to rib her hard for sure. "I—" Her heart smashed into her rib cage as the force of blue-violet eyes collided with her own. "Cam?"

He took a step forward, his entire frame seemingly filling up the small office, making it feel even tinier. Today, he was wearing a clean and pressed shirt, and his jaw was clean-shaven. "J.D.," he began, his voice hoarse. "I'm so—what in God's name are those?" he growled.

"What?" She blinked. "What are you talking about?"

Striding past her, he stomped over to her desk. "These." His eyes blazed, and the temperature in the room dropped a few degrees.

"F-flowers," she stammered.

The expression on his face turned murderous. "Who sent them?"

She gaped at him. Was he crazy? "What are you talking about?"

A vein in his neck strained. "Who. Sent. Them?"

"You did," she said. "I mean, didn't you?"

"No," he replied. "I did not."

"Are you sure?"

"I bloody well am."

She held up the card to him. "Who else would write this? It—hey!"

He snatched the card and read it. "There's no name."

"No shit, Sherlock." She scratched at her chin. *Guess he didn't send the teddy bear either*. "But if you didn't send them, who did?"

"Well, I'm going to find out." Turning to the arrangement, he dug through the bouquet, ripping out greenery and roses. "There has to be some kind of receipt or something around here."

"Hey!" She pushed him away. "Stop that! You're destroying them!"

"Oh, and you care about them now? Who are they really from? Some lover or—"

"Oh geez, calm the fuck down, Spenser." She rolled her eyes. "As if I was the type to attract this kind of attention." *Maybe someone like Darcey would get anonymous flowers*, she wanted to say aloud but held her tongue. "It doesn't have my name on it either so *obviously* there's been a mistake. Some poor delivery guy fucked up. A very expensive fuck up, too, considering how much roses cost this time of the year."

That was the most logical explanation, but she couldn't help the disappointment when she realized Cam didn't sent the flowers. "What are you doing here, anyway?"

"I ..." He swallowed hard. "J.D., I wanted to speak with you."

"You do, huh?" She crossed her arms over her chest and leaned her hip on the desk. "What about?" *And why did it take you this long to come to me?*

"I'm sorry," he blurted out. "For getting all caught up and forgetting to call you. I hope ... I hope you allow me to explain."

Part of her wanted to kick him out and yell that it was too late. But who the fuck was she kidding? And how could she turn him away when he looked like *that*? Like he was really, truly sorry. Even her cat felt his sincerity. It nosed at her, as if urging her to listen to him.

Her eyes flickered over to her father's framed photo. Pop always said, *If a man can swallow his pride to come to you hat in hand, the least you can do is hear him out.* "All right then, Spenser. *Talk.*"

Chapter 8

When J.D. ran out of his office last Monday, the first thing Cam thought was, *This is why I avoid relationships*. He was damn terrible at them, and there was no use trying to reason with an unreasonable creature such as a woman. He'd studied animals more agreeable and less easily agitated, like wolverines and honey badgers.

But, then again, he knew he'd been in the wrong. He *should* have called her. But he didn't lie to her, not intentionally.

After his conversation with his grandmother, he couldn't sleep. This whole thing was such a big, looming cloud that it was the only thing he could think of. He kept analyzing it from every angle, when would be the best time to tell J.D. about him leaving, how to tell her, and anticipate her reactions so he could mitigate them.

It was all too much, and he had gone through some kind of paralysis, unable to move on any action because any decision he made would leave either her, him, or his grandmother unhappy.

Work always helped him relax and clear his head. So, he went straight to HQ. Time passed, he had vague memories of seeing other people, making meals in the communal kitchen, crashing in the dorm, and heading out into the forest to check in on some of the subjects he'd been observing the past few months.

Out there, in his polar bear form, he didn't have to think about family responsibilities and the thought of making J.D. unhappy, but it also left him exhausted. Really exhausted, to the point of not keeping track of time. He truly thought only a few hours, a day at most, had passed when she came storming into his office.

She had acted so unreasonable that day, going on about her bloody tree and Christmas. He told himself he was happy she left and he didn't have to deal with her anymore. But his damned polar bear fought him at every turn, wouldn't let him rest, wanting to see her, to make things right with her. It was only because of sheer exhaustion that he was able to stay away from her. He was surprised he lasted this long, because when he woke up this morning, he found that he just couldn't let things stay this way.

But now, where to begin? With an apology, he supposed.

"Well?" She tapped her foot impatiently. "I'm waiting."

Right. He cleared his throat. "J.D., I truly am sorry. I was going to call you, but I got caught up. I really wanted to spend the day with you."

She sniffed. "Sure didn't feel like it. Especially when you lied to me."

"Lied to you? About—" Her warning glare made his clamp his mouth shut. *Damn.* "You're right. I mean, I didn't tell you the whole truth, so it was a lie by omission."

"Why did you do it?"

"I was afraid."

"Afraid? Of what?"

His throat threatened to collapse, but try as he might, he couldn't manage the words. Sweat formed on his temples and his chest contracted, that crushing feeling making it difficult to move or breathe. He looked at her, pleading with his eyes. *Please, J.D.*

Her head cocked to the side, brows drawing together, as if she was analyzing him. Then, it was like something clicked and she took a step toward him, her hand reaching out to cup the side of his face. Those hauntingly beautiful hazel eyes bore into him. "You really are afraid, aren't you? Of what?"

Closing his eyes, he nuzzled at her palm, breathing in her comforting scent. "Of losing you. You see, despite the very short time we've known each other, I can't quite imagine my life without you."

She sucked in a breath, and her hands slapped over her mouth. Time ticked by and flowed, while they remained stuck in that moment, staring at each other.

Finally, she lowered her hands to her sides. "I gotta hand it to you, champ," she said as her grin widened. "You have a way with words."

His breath caught in his lungs. "So ... you forgive me?"

She raised a blonde brow. "Not quite there yet. And you still owe me an explanation."

"Right. I just don't know where to begin. And there are so many details ... we need to sit down and ..." He ran his fingers through his hair. "And even then ... you still might change your mind about me."

"How about you just start with the basics, and you can fill

in the details later? What was so important that you forgot about me? Just start with what's really bothering you."

"All right." *Just the important details then.* "After I dropped you off, I got a call from my grandmother."

"Your grandma calls you? How sweet."

"Yeah. She's ... special." He swallowed the lump in his throat. "Except for my younger half sister, she's really the only family I have left. My grandmother lives in Europe and splits her time between London and Russia."

"Russia?"

"Yes. My maternal family's from there, and my father was English. It's complicated, but my parents didn't get along that much through most of their marriage." That was probably putting it mildly. "My mum died when I was six. Car crash. Killed on impact."

She sucked in a breath. "Cam, I'm sorry."

"It's all right, I don't remember her much." Only the stuff his father would scream at him whenever he was in his cups.

Whore cunt! She was with one of her lovers when they careened that sports car off that cliff. Damned bitch deserved it.

"Cam."

Her voice jolted back to the present. "Anyway, when I was old enough, I was sent to boarding school. Didn't see much of my father, but when I could leave for the summer, I would always spend it with my grandparents."

"They took care of you," she concluded. "And your grandmother was probably like your mother."

"Yes." Natalia was the only maternal figure he knew growing up. "But they weren't that benevolent. The truth was, I was being groomed."

"Groomed?"

"To take over the family interests back in Europe." He struggled trying to figure out what to say and how much to say. Because if she found out the truth about *that* side of his family, she might look at him differently. "And well, the thing is, it's always been understood that I would be taking over the ... the business. Sure, my grandmother indulged me when I said I wanted to pursue my scientific studies and research first, but always with the caveat that when it was time, I would take over. I thought I had more time, but then my grandfather passed away unexpectedly. And well ... time pretty much ran out a year ago, but I begged my grandmother to give me another year."

"Wait ... so you're here temporarily?"

The distress in her voice made his polar bear growl. "I had to finish one more paper to complete my second PhD, and then this opportunity came up to do more research here in exchange for field work with the rangers." He raked his hands through his hair. "I really was planning to go back. And then ... I met you.

"I was so caught up with the whole mating thing and then she called me to remind me that my time here was ending. I don't want to leave you, J.D., but I couldn't disappoint her either. I panicked. I tried to find a solution, but every hypothetical scenario left everyone unhappy. So, I went to work, trying to clear my head and then hours passed and—"

"Cam." She gripped his forearms. "Hey, c'mon now. Breathe."

He didn't realize his lungs had been running on empty. "J.D. ... I'm sorry for not telling you sooner. I wanted to work out a solution first. I couldn't just leave you, but I couldn't ignore my obligations back home either." His grandmother's life literally depended on it. "And I thought you could come with me, but I couldn't take you away from everything you've known."

Her mouth opened. "So that's it? You got stuck in some kind of analysis paralysis loop and just kind of ... short-circuited?"

Huh. It was a funny way to put it, but he couldn't have described it better himself. "I suppose so. But it all seemed hopeless. I mean, what are we supposed to do? Your friends ... they're all mated and happy, and I just want that for us too."

"Oh, baby." She wrapped her arms around him and lay her cheek on his chest. "I wish you said something sooner. But ..." Taking a deep breath, she lifted her head and looked him square in the eyes. "Cam, this whole thing between us ... I know we're fated mates and the universe or God or whatever says we're meant to be together forever, but really, we're still just two different people, trying to figure out how we fit together. We can't compare ourselves to Damon and Anna Victoria or Gabriel and Temperance. You're you and I'm me and we're *us*. There aren't any rules to mating, are there? One that says one of us has to give everything up for the other? I mean, it's not like we're getting married tomorrow. You were the one who wanted to take things slow, right?"

She had a point there. "But what do we do then?"

"Well ... we don't have to decide now, right? When you do have to go back?"

"My contract with the rangers expires at the end of the year, so January at the latest."

"All right." She chewed at her lip. "Well, the long-distance thing will suck, but people do it all the time. We can plan for it, and maybe we can come up with some compromise. I mean, your family business back in Europe isn't something you need to be there all the time for, right? Like, do you guys have a turnip farm or nesting doll factory or something?"

"Er ... nothing like that." He was tempted to tell her, but the rest of the details about his family was something he would have to ease her into. "Are you saying you're willing to make this work? With me leaving, that is?"

"Well, duh. You're my mate." Smiling up at him, she wrapped her arms around his neck. "And you've got a full head of hair, complete teeth, and I wanna bone you again."

He threw his head back and laughed, the weight suddenly lifting from his chest and shoulders. "Well ... if you insist." He bent down to hook his hands under her knees, then lifted her up, backing her toward the desk.

"Cam, I—oops!" When he planted her on top of the desk, her back hit the vase of flowers, sending it crashing down.

"Fucking flowers," he growled.

She rolled her eyes. "I told you, it was probably a wrong delivery."

Occam's Razor demanded that he accept the simplest possible explanation for the existing data. However, the primal, animal part of him demanded to know who would *dare* send their mate gifts. Then hunt them down and let them know it was inappropriate. Preferably using his teeth and claws.

"Cam ..." she said in a warning tone.

"Fine," he grumbled.

"You're so cute when you're jealous," she chuckled.

"Jealousy is an illogical reaction. I do *not* get jealous."

"Right." She patted him on the shoulder and kissed his nose. "Now, as much as I do wanna play hide the cannoli with you again, I've got a garage full of employees with shifter senses. I'll never hear the end of it if they hear us doing it in here. Not to mention, I don't think I can keep my lady juices flowing with my dad looking down at us." She nodded at the portrait hanging on the wall behind the desk.

"I suppose we should stop desecrating offices." *Sorry about that, sir,* he silently said to the smiling man in the picture. He could see the resemblance, and now he knew where she got her stubborn chin and stunning eyes from. "I like the rest of the decor." Glancing around, he took note of the eclectic collection of memorabilia and knickknacks. "James Dean? And Billy Joel, huh?"

"Oh yeah, my old man *loved* him. Ever see that video where he's in the mechanic shop and that gorgeous blonde pulls up in the 1958 Rolls-Royce Silver Wraith? He was so tickled pink by it and he always called Ma his Uptown Girl, even though she grew up in Jersey City. Anyway"—she hopped down off the table—"why don't we get outta here?"

"Of course. But ... have you forgiven me yet?"

"Duh," she said. "But you still have to make it up to me."

"I do?"

"Yes." She took his hands into hers. "Come with me to the Christmas Carnival at Lennox Park."

"When?"

"Now. They're going to turn on all the lights soon."

"Now?" His first instinct was to say no. How could he explain that his feelings regarding the holidays were the complete opposite of hers? The scores of happy families around them would only remind him how glum his Christmases were.

What day are you fetching me for the Christmas holiday, Father?

I'm afraid that's not possible, Cameron. You'll have to stay put for now.

Oh. Maybe next year?

Perhaps.

But, knowing how much she loved Christmas and what it meant to her—not to mention how understanding she'd been despite the fact that he'd left her alone for days *and* she was still willing to take him back *and* find a solution to their logistical problem—he knew he could bear one night surrounded by the trappings of this godforsaken holiday. "All right."

"Really?" Seeing her eyes light up and her body practically vibrate with excitement made him and his bear glow with pleasure. "Great! The Christmas Carnival is so awesome! You'll love it, I swear! Let me get my coat."

Chapter 9

Lucas Lennox Park was already teeming with crowds gathered for the beginning of the Winter Carnival when they arrived

"Lennox Corp. goes all out during the holiday," J.D. explained as they made their way to the center of the park. "They get the whole place lit up, and they have a huge Christmas tree and everything."

"Like Rockefeller Center in New York City?" he asked.

"Yeah," she said. "We used to go every December. Ma and Pop and me, I mean. It was our tradition. When Pop and I moved here, we were kinda glad they had this. It was like having a piece of her come over with us, you know?" She took in a deep breath and closed her eyes remembering all those good memories. Any other time of the year, the loss of her parents only made her sad, but during the holidays, it was as if she could feel their presence in the air. It was a consoling feeling.

"So, where's your spot?"

She blinked at him. "My spot?"

He let out an exaggerated sigh. "Tut-tut. You're no amateur, are you, McNamara? Surely over the years you've curated the best spot for the tree lighting ceremony?"

How did he know? "Of course. C'mon."

She dragged him across the park, not toward the large tree and stage set up in the middle, but up a small hill on the east side. They trudged up a path until they reached the top, which offered them a view of the park below.

"It's starting," she said.

The Christmas music piping in through loud speakers faded away, and the people cheered and clapped as an emcee came onstage to start the festivities.

"... and now, let's welcome our benefactor and honored guest, CEO of Lennox Corporation, Mr. Matthew Lennox, to say a few words before he officially opens the Blackstone Winter Carnival."

Though they were far away, she could make out Matthew as he came on stage, his wife Catherine by his side, carrying their son, Devon. The dragon shifter said a few words, made a joke or two, then finally, declared the carnival open.

A dazzling display exploded in front of them as the lights turned on, starting from the fifty-foot tall tree in the center and then spreading out across the entire park.

"It's so beautiful," she whispered.

A pair of strong arms came around her, and Cam rested his chin on top of her head. With a contented sigh, she sank back against him, allowing his warmth and scent to surround her. Her cat purred contentedly.

Turning around, she pressed herself up against him, then looked up into his blue-violet eyes. His chest rumbled as he bent his head down.

God, I've missed this so much, she thought as their lips touched. Which was impossible because it had only been a week since their last kiss, but it was as if she'd been starving for his lips for years. His firm mouth moved over hers in a gentle caress, his arms tightening around her. *Tonight,* she thought. She had to have him tonight or she'd go crazy. But first ...

"Everything okay?" he panted when she pulled away. "Didn't you like it—"

"Oh yes, I did." She nipped at his lip. "But ... we need to go down to the carnival, now!"

Grabbing his hand, she tugged him back toward the park. They laughed and giggled like teenagers as they made their way to the main carnival area where there were various booths set up as well as food trucks, concession stands, a skating rink, and even a carousel and Ferris wheel.

"What would you like to do first?" he asked.

"Everything," she laughed. "C'mon."

They went to the rink first, and J.D. couldn't help but crack jokes about polar bears and ice skating, especially when Cam fell down twice. Then they lined up for the Ferris wheel where they made out the entire time, and afterward, checked out some of the craft booths. Cam, despite being grumpy because she wanted to look at every stall, insisted on buying her every ornament she glanced at.

"I'm starving," she declared. "But I also want you to win me a stuffed animal at the games." The carnival always overwhelmed her, but having Cam with her this year made her extra excited. "And—oh look! I think I see Jason and Christina Lennox." She pointed toward the Christmas tree where the younger of the Lennox dragon twins was standing with his mate. "Geez, she looks ready to pop," she noted, seeing Christina's protruding pregnant belly. "Let's go say hi."

"Uh ..." Cam stuck a finger in his collar and pulled at it. "How about you go and say hello, and I'll get us some food and drinks. Then afterward, we can check out the games, and I can win you the biggest stuffed animal they have."

"Ooh!" She clapped her hands together. "I have my eye on that purple dragon at the milk can game." Leaping up, she kissed him on the cheek. "All right, champ. I'll meet you there, okay?"

He seemed oddly relieved. "Yes. And, J.D.?"

"Yes?"

"Afterward ... tonight ..."

"Yes." She winked at him. "Why do you think I let you drive and left my car at the garage?" She already knew they wouldn't be needing two cars to go their separate ways tonight.

Desire glittered in his eyes. "Yes, that too. But ... we should also talk about other things. More ... details you should know before we ..."

"Cam," she began and curved her hand on his cheek. "Unless you're going to tell me you're a homicidal maniac, there's nothing you can say that would make me not want you."

Earlier in her office, she had seen the signs of fear and anxiety on his face and body language. She had recognized it because Damon had been like that when he came home from the Special Forces, though Cam's case was mild compared to her best friend's PTSD. When she dealt with it, she had figured out that it was best for Damon to open up to her without any pressure and reveal only the pertinent details. "So, don't you sweat the small stuff, okay?"

Closing his eyes, he covered her hand with his and kissed her palm. "I don't deserve you."

The butterflies in her stomach fluttered. "Oh, you ... now go get my food," she said, playfully pushing him away. With one last smile, he turned and walked toward the concession stands.

She stood there, watching him disappear into the crowd, anticipation making her giddy for tonight. Her cat mewled impatiently, but she told it everything would be worth it.

Whirling around, she frowned as she realized that Jason and Christina were no longer where she last spotted them. *Maybe they walked around to the other side.* Shrugging, she strode toward the display. *Even if I don't get to see them, I haven't seen the tree yet and—*"Hey!" Someone brushed past her, making her tumble forward. As she wobbled to regain her balance, hands grabbed her to steady her. "Thanks —*oomph!*"

The wind whooshed out of her as she felt a blow to her abdomen, sending pain shooting through her. Her feet lifted off the ground, then everything turned upside-down.

Shock and confusion paralyzed her. Her cat, on the other hand, hissed at her to *get it together*.

"What the fuck!" she shouted. "Is this a joke?"

Something was stuffed into her mouth to prevent her from speaking, then her vision went dark as she felt rough cloth go over her head. Her brain's synapses shot off, trying to make sense of what happened because this was not a joke. She was getting kidnapped.

She struggled to get free, but the grip around her

tightened. Her body bounced as her kidnapper picked up his pace. It was difficult to get the air back in her lungs as an obstruction blocked her nostrils each time she tried to breath in. *They put some kind of hood over my head.* It was disorienting, to have her vision impaired while being upside-down, but she managed to unsheathe her claws, then raked it over the first thing she could reach.

"Oww!" Her kidnapper screamed as her claws dug into flesh. "Bitch!" The bouncing halted.

"Goddammit, Murray, why the hell are you stopping? We gotta get—"

"Damn bitch has claws!"

You're Goddamn right I have claws!

"Tie her up!"

Oh no you don't! Her only escape was to shift into her cat.

"Get away from her!"

There was a shout, followed by the sound of a scuffle. She was preparing to shift when she felt her body drop to the ground. Her elbows and knees hit the ground, shooting pain up her limbs.

"Bitch! You'll pay for scratching me up!" A booted foot slammed up into her face, sending her reeling onto her back.

"Bastard! Get the fuck away from her!"

She was still in a daze, but the pain in her jaw slowly brought her back. It took her another second, but she finally oriented herself. Whipping the hood off, she got to her feet and spit out the fabric stuffed in her mouth. *"Blech!"* Blood tasted like iron on her tongue.

"J.D., are you all right?"

Lifting her head, she stared up into the familiar face of

Roy Jorrell. "R-Roy? What are you doing here? Oh my God, you've been hurt!"

There was a deep cut on his cheekbone. "'S nothing," he snorted, rubbing the blood off with the back of his hand. "Are you all right? I thought I saw you back there, and then those guys came out of nowhere and—" Anger blazed in his eyes. "Those fucking bastards *hurt you*."

Her entire jaw was on fire, and she spit out the blood pooling in her mouth. "Oh ... fuck!" Adrenaline seeped out of her system, and her muscles went limp. Roy caught her as she staggered forward. Her cat didn't like that and swiped its claws at him. "Th-they tried to ... what did you see?"

His arms tightened around her as he pressed his cheek to hers. "I was on my way to check out the Christmas tree when I thought I spotted you. Then these two guys come out from nowhere and picked you up, then ran off. I thought ... I went after them and tackled one of the guys."

"Thank God you saw me."

"Why would they do that?" he asked.

"I don't know. But—" A thought popped into her head.

A couple weeks back, she and Dutchy had unwittingly stumbled upon a shifter poaching operation in the mountains. The perpetrators captured her and Dutchy, but she was able to escape by shifting and got help. Krieger had killed all of the poachers, and Jason and Christina, who ran the Shifter Protection Agency of Blackstone, found the rest of the shifters they had kidnapped. "I need to go find someone."

"Go find—J.D., you were almost kidnapped!" Roy's grip tightened on her. "Why don't you let me help you get calmed down, and then maybe we can—"

"Look, I appreciate you coming to my rescue, I really do,

Roy." She pried herself away from him. "But there could be bigger things at play here."

"B-bigger things?" His expression became inscrutable.

"Yeah. Again, thank you, but I need to go find Jason and Christina Lennox. You go and enjoy the carnival." Her cat very much agreed with that, wanting to get away from him *and* clean off the stench of his feathers from their body. *Why are you such a drama queen?* she scolded her cat. *He helped us, for crying out loud.*

The feline wrinkled its nose and let out what sounded like a *hmph* sound as it whipped its tail.

Weirdo.

"I'll help you find them," he offered.

She very much wished he had said otherwise, but she couldn't waste any more time. "All right, let's go."

It turned out her kidnappers didn't get her very far. They had veered off the main path, into the thicket surrounding the park. *Hmmm.* Where would they have taken her, though? They couldn't have hidden a car there. Maybe a motorcycle? And why wouldn't they try to drug her first? It just didn't quite add up.

She dashed back toward the tree, but didn't see any sign of Jason or Christina.

"Who are we looking for?" Roy asked as he came up beside her.

"You're still here?" She couldn't stop herself from saying it aloud. "I mean ... I'm looking for ... Jason!" There he was, along with Christina, standing by the skating rink. There was also a third person with them. *Cam!*

Her inner cat urged her to go to him. Not that she needed any more encouragement. Her feet practically flew off the ground as she raced to her mate and launched herself at him.

"... said she was coming to meet you, but—J.D.? *Oomph!*"

"Cam," she breathed, rubbing her face against his shirt. "Oh, Cam."

"Where were you?" He gently pried her away. "I—" The expression on his face changed from relief to confusion and then anger. "What the fuck—you're hurt." Blue-violet eyes filled with rage as he gently cupped her jaw.

"It's already healing," she assured him. "But I need to—" Remembering why she was looking for them in the first place, she turned to Jason and Christina. "Thank God you guys are here."

"J.D., what happened?" Christina asked, a mask of concern on her face. "Cam said you were coming to say hi to us."

"I was." She frowned, then turned to Cam. "I thought you were going to wait by the milk can game."

"I was." His jaw tensed. "But I ... I changed my mind and wanted to say hello to Jason and Christina as well. What the hell happened?"

"She was kidnapped," Roy said. "I saw it happen."

"Kidnapped?" The fury from Cam and his animal radiated off him in waves. "And who are you?" he asked in a murderous tone.

"Cam, please." *Oh boy.* "This is Roy. We went to school together and—"

"I'm the guy who rescued her," Roy snarled back. "Who the hell are *you*?"

"Her mate," he growled possessively as he took a step forward.

Shock and confusion crossed Roy's face. "You're—"

"Mate?" Jason finished, dark brows crinkling. "Oh, congratulations. No wonder you were going crazy when you couldn't find her."

Cam cleared his throat. "Can we talk about this later? Right now, we need to find out why someone would fucking dare hurt *my mate!*"

"That's why I was looking for you too," J.D. said to the other couple. "It could be the poachers."

"Poachers?" Roy and Cam said at the same time.

"Yeah, a while back, me and Dutchy—"

"J.D." Jason's warning, dominant tone made her snap her mouth shut. The meaningful look he shot her reminded her that she wasn't supposed to talk to anybody about the poaching incident. After all, The Shifter Protection Agency, which she herself had only found out about during the rescue, was supposed to be a secret.

Jason cleared his throat before addressing Roy. "So ... Roy, right? I'm Jason. Did you go to Lennox High?"

"Yeah, before I moved away in grade eight. Moved back a couple of weeks ago."

"Thanks for coming to her rescue, Roy. But don't worry, we'll take it from here now." Jason's tone was firm, the meaning behind it clear.

"But—"

"You've done so much, putting yourself in danger, and we can't risk you getting more involved. It's ... a family matter now," Jason insisted. "And we'd like to keep it private, if you don't mind."

Roy took a step toward her, provoking Cam to growl at him.

She placed a soothing hand on his arm. "Just give me a sec, okay?" Turning to Roy, she took a deep breath. "Thank you so much, Roy. For what you did. Who knows what would have happened if you weren't there." Her cat let out a miffed sniff, as if saying, *We can take care of ourselves.* "But ... I think Jason is right."

"If you'd like," Jason began, "I saw Deputy Carson right by the Ferris wheel. We can go over there and tell him what happened. But then he'll want all of us to come down to the station and conduct interviews and file a report ... and that could take all night."

"I, uh ..." Roy stammered. "I suppose you can get that all sorted with the authorities."

"My lawyer will take care of it," Jason assured him. "That's what I pay him for. Besides, maybe it was just some kids playing a stupid prank. Did you see who they were or what they looked like?"

"Um, yeah, I guess they could have been teenagers messing around. They were both wearing dark hoodies, boots, and jeans."

They didn't sound like kids. But J.D. kept that thought to herself because Jason was trying to throw Roy off.

"Let's exchange contact info," Jason said. "Christina, sweetheart, why don't you take J.D. to the Lennox Corp. VIP lounge and get her a drink?"

"Of course," she said. "Come with me."

"Wait." Roy turned to J.D. "Are you gonna be okay?"

Cam grit his teeth. "She's with me. Of course she'll be—"

She sent him a warning glare, then addressed Roy. "Yeah, I'll be fine. Thanks again. Next oil change is on me, okay?" She only hoped his next five thousand miles wasn't too soon.

"All right. Stay safe, J.D., and I'll see you around."

Before Cam could react, she tugged at his arm. "You said there was a lounge around here? And booze?" she asked Christina.

"Yeah," Christina said with a chuckle. "C'mon. Jason will join us once he's done with your friend."

Christina led them around the skating rink, back to where a large tent had been set up. Above the entrance was a sign with the logo of the Lennox Corporation. Upon seeing Christina, the burly guard at the front opened the flap to let them in.

"Wow," J.D. exclaimed as she drank in the surroundings. "So, this is how the other half lives."

Though it looked like any canvas tent from the outside, the inside was richly decorated, with plush carpets, leather seats, brass chandeliers overhead, and even a full-sized bar with a bartender in a white tuxedo mixing up drinks. There were a few people in the lounge, so Christina took them to a quiet corner where two leather couches were set up.

"Please, have a seat." She herself eased down on one of the couches, hand on her back as she let out a sigh. "*Whew*, my feet are killing me." Her hand landed on top of her pregnant belly.

"When are you due?" J.D. asked as she and Cam took the opposite couch.

"In two weeks," Christina answered. "Although I'm just about ready to send these guys an eviction notice."

"These guys? You're having twins?"

She nodded. "Yeah. And no, I don't recommend it." Turning to Cam, she asked, "You're not a twin, are you, Cam?"

"Uh, no."

"Thank your lucky stars," she joked to J.D. "Anyway, tell me what happened."

Taking a deep breath, she gave Christina as much details as she could recall. Of course, with each passing second, Cam only grew more and more agitated.

"Bloody blighters," Cam bit out. "Why are we sitting around here when we should be out there looking for those men who hurt you?"

"I'm already healing," J.D. pointed out. "And they didn't succeed."

"Not tonight," he countered. "What the hell are you going to do about this?" he asked Christina. "Are you even taking this seriously? Do you care that—"

J.D. gripped his arm. "Cam!"

Christina calmly raised a blonde brow at him. "I know you shifter males can be unreasonable when it comes to your mates, so I'll let that slide," she began. "But I can't cause a panic over two would-be kidnappers. We have private security all over the place and a few SPA agents going around incognito. Jason should be informing them of what happened by now, aided by your friend Roy's description."

"Who was that tosser anyway?" he asked J.D.

"Just a guy I went to high school with. And if he wasn't there—wait, are you jealous?"

"I told you, I do not get jealous," he harrumphed. "But I do not appreciate my mate coming to me stinking of another male's feathers."

J.D. shot to her feet. "What the hell are you insinuating, Spenser?"

"All right, all right, just calm down," Christina said wryly.

"J.D., sit before you send me into premature labor. Cam, I would suggest you put your shifter male ego aside and think before you open your mouth."

Crossing her arms over her chest, she sat back down, but scooted a few inches away from Cam. He didn't like that at all and made it known with a growl.

"Ugh, you two seriously need to work on the mate bond soon," Christina said.

"Will that make him stop acting like a possessive jerk?" J.D. asked.

"Not really," she said with a chuckle. "But maybe you won't mind so much."

"Oh great, you guys are here." Jason approached them from behind, then sat down next to Christina. "I took care of Roy. He told me his side of the story and I got his info. I'm not sure if it's valuable, but if we need to talk to him again, I can at least get a hold of him. Everyone on the team's been informed as well and is on the lookout."

"Thank you so much, Jason," J.D. said.

"I'm afraid there's not much else we can do," Christina said. "We don't have cameras set up here, and there's just so many people around. It would be like finding a needle in a haystack at this point."

"But rest assured, we'll do our best to find out where these guys are and prevent them from doing this again." Jason, however, was looking straight at Cam.

"That sounds great, thank you both." J.D. sank back into the plush couch.

"We should get going, I'm exhausted." Christina stood up slowly, Jason helping her. "The team will update us back home."

"I told you we shouldn't have come," Jason said. "You're supposed to be on maternity leave."

"You were driving me mad with your hovering," Christina shot back. "And I can't just stay in bed for two whole weeks. J.D, Cam, please stay here and enjoy the lounge."

"Food and drinks are free, and you know Lennox Corp. always serves the good stuff," he said with a chuckle. "Call us if you need anything, and J.D.?"

"Yes?"

"Welcome to the family, I guess?"

"Welcome to the—"

Cam cleared his throat. "Thank you. Both of you. We'll be in touch."

The couple strode away, leaving them alone. She was ready to do battle, but Cam surprised her by speaking first.

"I'm sorry, J.D.," he said. "When I couldn't find you, I went crazy. I didn't mean to insinuate that you and Roy were doing anything wrong."

His apology had somehow knocked her defenses down. "I was lucky he was there at the right time and the right place. I fell, and so of course, he helped me up. I was shocked and scared and he—"

"I know." His jaw clenched. "And that's what angered me. That *I* wasn't there to prevent those bastards from hurting you."

Oh, Cam. She scooted closer to him. "You can't be with me twenty-four seven. Sometimes, things just happen. And I'm tough, okay? Been taking care of myself for a long time, I could have shifted and escaped. Besides, if those guys had succeeded, I'm pretty sure you would have done anything you could to get me back."

"Nothing would have stopped me." His chest rumbled, and a growl from his bear rattled in his throat.

Her cat, the silly thing, swooned with giddiness. Arms came around her, then Cam pulled her onto his lap.

"We're not alone in here, you know," she said, eyes darting to the other people in the lounge.

"I don't care." He pulled her head down to meet his mouth in a rough, possessive kiss that stoked a fire in her. "J.D., I need you so bad. Need to be with you." The brush of his erection against her made her gasp. "Need to be inside you."

"Then what are we waiting for? Take me home, champ."

Chapter 10

Driving back to his penthouse took every ounce of concentration he had left. With J.D. right next to him, it was difficult not to just pull over to the side of the road and haul her onto his lap and have his way with her.

Perhaps the roller coaster of emotions from tonight had something to do with it, but he didn't care why. He wanted J.D. to be his, irrevocably. To bond with her and make her his forever.

Things at the carnival had been going marvelously at first. He still couldn't believe that despite everything he did and what she knew, J.D. still wanted to work things out.

And that's why he went into a panic when he saw Jason and Christina Lennox. They would recognize him, of course, and J.D. would have more questions. Coward that he was, he didn't want to think about the consequences of another lie of omission, so he escaped.

He was about halfway toward the game booths when he realized he owed her the truth. Not only about Natalia and his family obligations, but his connections to the Lennoxes that she would undoubtedly uncover anyway.

He sought out Jason and Christina, but they hadn't seen her at all. He didn't know why, but he started to panic. Then she showed up from out of nowhere, and when he saw she'd been hurt, his polar bear had gone crazy. And it didn't help that the other male had his scent all over her.

His bear chuffed, still miffed at him. *That man did save her*, he tried to reason, but his animal wouldn't hear any of it. No one touched their mate.

J.D. let out a whistle that jolted him out of his thoughts. "Nice digs," she said as they pulled up to his sleek and modern building.

I should tell her the truth.

His bear roared in protest, as if to say, *no. Mate now. Truth later.*

"It's a rental," he mumbled as he went into the garage and pulled into his spot. When he turned off the engine, he turned to her. "J.D., I—"

"Shush!" She pressed a finger to his lips. "If you're going to ask me if I've changed my mind, I haven't."

"Yes, but—"

"Spenser, I swear to God, if you don't take me up to your place now, I'm going to—"

Wrapping his hand around the back of her head, he pulled her in for a deep kiss. "All right," he breathed as he pressed his forehead to hers. "Let's go."

He led her to the elevators and up to his floor, then dragged her to his door. As soon as it opened, he pushed her inside and kissed her, not bothering to turn on any lights as they could both see in the dark anyway.

Their hands fumbled at each other's clothing, as if competing on who could undress who first. Jackets, shirts, and trousers were left in a trail across the hardwood floor. Scooping her up into his arms, he was about to head to the bedroom but decided it was too far and so deposited her on the massive sectional couch in the living room. Putting his glasses aside, he knelt in front of her and pushed her knees apart. God, her smell was intoxicating, and he couldn't help himself as he slipped his hands under her ass and hauled her to his mouth.

"Cam!" she cried out as he mouthed her through the damp cotton of her panties. He teased her, running his tongue along the nearly transparent fabric that showed off the outline of her slick lips.

Hooking his finger along one side of her underwear, he exposed her so he could taste her naked pussy, the juices wetting his lips and chin, the thatch of blonde curls tickling his nose. *Lord, I could do this all day.* Her sweet nectar would be all he needed to survive.

Her hips lifted up, so he helped her by slipping her panties off to give him better access. "That's a good girl," he said as her thighs parted wider. He slipped a finger in her and had her whimpering and squirming in minutes. "Come, love," he said, before leaning forward to clamp his mouth around her engorged clit.

"*Nggghh!*" Fingers grabbed at his hair and pulled as her body shook with her orgasm. He lapped at her as he continued to fuck her with his finger, wanting to feel her clamping around him. His cock went hard as steel, throbbing and aching in want.

With a grunt, he lifted her up again, turned around, and

sat back on the couch. As her legs moved to straddle him, he pulled her bra cups down to expose her breasts. He cupped them, and she shivered as his thumbs rubbed her large nipples to hardness. Unable to help himself, he took one in his mouth. Fuck, they tasted even better than he'd remembered.

He continued to tease her nipples with his tongue, switching sides to give them equal attention. J.D. was practically melting in his lap, her naked pussy rubbing over his erection, making the front of his briefs wet with her juices.

"Goddammit, Cam, I need you to fuck me now," she groaned. "Need that magnificent cock of yours in me ... ohhh!" She let out a yelp when he gave her left nipple a gentle nip. "Stop teasing ..."

"Hmmm." Pulling away from her nipples, he brushed a thumb over her lower lip. "Such a dirty pretty mouth you have. I bet you could do so many more things with it than talk."

"Only things you can dream of, champ."

He attempted to dip his thumb into her mouth, but she responded with a nip of her teeth. "Are you going to make me earn this pretty mouth?"

"What do you think?"

The defiant look in her eyes made him want her even more. "Oh, I'll have you on your knees and that mouth on my cock," he growled. "You'll beg me for it."

"Fuck, you quiet types always have the dirtiest mouths, don't you?" She was practically panting as she reached between them to take his cock out of his underwear, and he helped her by lifting his hips. But he barely had his underwear down to his knees when she pointed the tip of his cock at her entrance.

"J. ... D.!" he moaned as she sank down on him slowly. Her grip around him was like a vice, and it took all his energy and focus not to lose control right then and there. "Love ... please."

She let out a triumphant little sigh as she finally took him all in. "So ... full. How the heck did we ..."

"You were made for me," he crooned into her hair as he placed his hands on her hips. "So good."

"Cam," she purred. "Oh, Cam." Her hips began to move. Slowly, but tentatively, in a slow rhythm that would surely drive him mad. And he didn't care. He was mad—crazy for her.

As she pistoned up and down, her pace quickening, he kissed every inch of her he could reach. Her face, her neck, those spectacular nipples that haunted his dreams. She seemed to enjoy it as she gripped his shoulders. When he bit at her neck, she let out a snarl, her nails digging painfully into his flesh as she squeezed around him tighter. God, she was unlike anything he'd experienced before. But he needed more. The primal, base urge inside him needed to show her who was in charge around here.

A surprised yelp escaped her mouth as he flipped her over without withdrawing. He pinned her to the couch, hands gripping her wrists as he put them over her head. She let out a savage growl, but that only spurred him more. Putting her wrists together with one hand, he kept her restrained, while his free hand roamed lower, teasing her breasts and abdomen until they reached his intended destination. He plucked at her clit and she let out a howl which he captured with his mouth as he moved in and out of her with a ferocious intensity he'd never displayed before.

He wanted her—all of her. Her sweet body, her surrender. The little minx wasn't giving up so easily, which he loved. She thrust her hips up at him, like he wasn't already fucking her hard, and her teeth nipped at him. God, she was a treasure. It only made him thrust harder into her, her moans and cries filling the room.

She was no longer fighting him, and instead, worked with him, their bodies in complete rhythm, reaching for that peak they both wanted. Nails scratched down his back so deeply it would surely leave marks. Her wrists would be bruised from the way he held her so tight, but neither cared. Because they were so close.

"Cam!" she burst out as her body began to shudder.

He held on as long as he could so he could watch her reach the peak. It was a thing of beauty, to see her eyes close, face twist in pleasure, her head thrown back, her tight passage squeezing him as she came. When she opened those beautiful, passion-filled eyes and stared up at him, that's when he lost it. The pressure that had been building up in his body released, the pleasure zinging up his spine and directly to his brain. His orgasm hit him so hard he lost feeling in his limbs for a second, every nerve ending fried as it concentrated on his groin. He held on to her as tight as he could, trying to ride out the wave as she squeezed her muscles tight around him. For a moment, he thought he had truly died and gone to heaven.

He must have fallen on top of her, because when he regained his senses, their bodies were plastered together.

Though he had dominated her in those last moments, he wondered who truly conquered whom.

"Cam? Would you mind ...?"

Reluctantly, he separated from her, his cock softening as he pulled out of her. J.D.'s body slick with sweat and thighs painted with his seed was a sight he would never forget, and hopefully, something he would see again.

"I—hey!" she chuckled as he pulled her up for a long, languid kiss. "Hmmm ... that was something."

"Indeed," he murmured against her mouth. "Um, let me get some towels to refresh us. Or would you like to take a shower?"

"Shower? Why go through the trouble when we're going to get sweaty again anyway," she said slyly looking down at his cock, which was now half hard again just from their kiss.

God, he wanted her again. Wanted her more than anything. "Good point. Let me get those towels and we can go to the bedroom."

He headed to the guest bathroom and grabbed the two hand towels hanging on the rack. When he came out to the living room, he saw that she was no longer on the couch. Instead, she had put on his shirt and stood by the baby grand piano in the corner of the living room, her fingers running over the ivory keys.

"It came with the apartment," he said.

"Oh, so you don't play?"

"Well ..." Striding over to her, he sat down on the bench, then pulled her to his lap, arms on either side of her. "The opportunity to work in here came at such short notice, so I had no choice but to find a flat online before I got here. It didn't matter to me which one, but the piano definitely cemented my decision to rent this one." His fingers landed on the keys, as he began to play the very first piece he'd learned "Twinkle Twinkle Little Star."

"Wow," she said, leaning back into him. "You're good."

"My grandparents insisted I learn during the summers spent with them, among other things. Chess, languages, different sports. They wanted to make sure I received a well-rounded education." He switched to a more complicated piece, one of his favorites: Liebesträum No. 3 in A-flat Major by Franz Liszt.

"That's so beautiful." She rubbed the side of her cheek against his arm. "But so sad. Do you know anything happier?"

He smiled to himself, then transitioned to Mozart's Piano Sonata No. 16 in C Major, following it with "Flight of the Bumblebee" just for fun, which was a feat considering she was between his arms, but he managed to finish the piece.

Turning in his lap, she straddled him so they came face-to-face. "Show off." She smirked at him. "Do you know anything from the last century?"

"Ah, that I can do." He kissed her nose, then put his fingers to the keys again and tinkled out an intro that he hoped she would recognize.

Instantly, her mouth formed a perfect O, and her breath hitched. "That's my dad's favorite song," she breathed, her eyes shimmering. "New York State of Mind."

"I figured it would be." It wasn't hard to figure out, with the posters in the office, but he was glad that he, as the Americans would say, nailed it.

Silently, she wound her arms around him and lay her cheek on his shoulder. He continued playing until he finished the song, and silence filled the room when the last echo faded. They sat there, unmoving, listening to the sound of each other's breathing and heartbeats.

"Thank you," she finally said. "That was ... amazing."

"You're welcome."

"You don't sing, do you?" she asked, pulling away and looking up at him. "Because that would be so unfair."

He laughed, then moved his hands from the piano to her thighs, pressing them tight around his waist before standing up.

"Where are we going?"

He maneuvered them around the piano and began to walk toward the direction of the master bedroom. "As much as I want to admire your naked bottom as you're bent over that magnificent instrument, I'd also like to see what it's like to make love to you on a proper mattress."

She laughed. "All right, Romeo. Take me to your bed."

Waking with J.D. every day for an entire week was perhaps the best feeling in the world. It was even better this morning, because neither of them worked today, he could quietly admire her without worrying about having to get up and get ready. She looked gorgeous, all that messy curly hair spilled over his arm as her nose nuzzled at his side, the curves of her body fitting perfectly into him. He loved to watch her, trace his eyes over her perfect skin and the green ink of the leaves curling around her bicep. When he'd asked her about it, she didn't hesitate to tell him that she'd gotten it in memory of her beloved mother, Ivy. After her father died, she added a few vines that spelled out "J.D.", which had also been his initials.

There was a contentment inside him he'd never felt before. His polar bear, too, let out a satisfied rumble.

Yes, this was all worth it. Even doing all the Christmas stuff with her. J.D. just about tried his patience, wanting to go to the Winter Carnival nearly every night, gorging on sweet and fried snacks, buying all kinds of Christmas ornaments that they would eventually hang on the already heaving tree at her house. When she ran out of space on her tree, she insisted on getting him one. Though he was resistant at first, he eventually relented and allowed her to put one up in his living room, and they decorated it together.

However, lurking in the back of his mind was that *one thing* he still hadn't told her about, despite spending every free moment he had with her. His bear snorted. It didn't want him to rock the boat, especially since the bond had not yet formed, and there was a possibility they could still lose her.

But when would the bond happen, exactly? He wondered if he could interview Damon and Gabriel to find out more about how they formed the bond with their respective mates.

"You're ... thinking too loudly ... for this early in the morning," J.D. said, yawning between phrases.

"It's ten in the morning," he pointed out.

"On a Saturday." With a long, languid *hmmmm,* she sat up slowly, stretching her limbs like a cat. Getting on her hands and knees, she leaned back, eyes hooded as they locked gazes. She was unabashed in her nakedness, hands crawling up her torso, over her breasts and nipples before raising them over her head for one long, glorious stretch.

Her nipples were practically begging for his attention, so he pounced on her, eliciting a half shout, half yell that didn't quite sound indignant. In fact, she was soon mewling in delight as he covered her body with his, his mouth teasing her left nipple.

"Cam," she purred, a sound that shot straight to his groin and made him instantly hard. "Mmmm, yes. Please."

Flipping her over to her stomach, he hauled that gorgeous ass up as he entered her in one smooth motion. "Wet already, are we?"

"I was dreaming of you," she moaned as he slid a hand between her thighs to play with her clit. "Of this."

He moved inside her, enjoying the grip of her pussy around him. Her moans and cries filled his ears, and he wanted this to last, but dammit, she felt too good. He rubbed her clit between his fingers just the way she liked it, and she shot to orgasm like a rocket. The tight squeeze of her narrow passage around him set him off, too, and he came hard, filling her with his seed.

"Oh wow," she moaned into the sheets. "What a way to wake up."

He smiled to himself. "Just what the doctor ordered, huh?"

Her body shook with laughter. "C'mon. Let's shower."

Of course, that was just an excuse to see her naked body wet and sudsy. He took her again, pressed up against the tile wall in his luxurious shower.

"I'm hungry," she declared as they toweled off.

"You're always hungry," he pointed out.

"And whose fault is that?"

"Entirely mine," he said. "I take full credit."

"You also never have food around here."

In the last week, they'd been splitting time between his

flat and her house, and J.D. kept complaining about his empty larder. He had explained to her that he rarely spent time here and thus saw no need to stock any food items.

"You were the one who insisted on spending the weekend here because you wanted to 'get railed hard' on the piano," he pointed out. And so she did, last night after they finished decorating the tree.

She chortled. "All right, let's go get some food, then I really should head over to Blackstone Bodyworx and go to a late yoga class with Anna Victoria and the girls." The chief's mate ran a fitness studio in South Blackstone. "I already missed last week."

After getting dressed, they drove down to Main Street. Being Saturday and with the holiday season in full swing, the streets were bustling with crowds. For once, Cam didn't mind the trappings of the holiday season, especially seeing J.D. all giddy with happiness, though that smug part of him wanted to believe *he* was the reason for that. The wait for Rosie's was long, but it was well worth it, especially as today's special included mincemeat pie. After lunch, they headed to South Blackstone.

While J.D. attended her yoga class, he went to the cafe to do some work. In the last week, he'd been clocking in and out at a more regular schedule so he could spend his nights with J.D., which meant he hadn't put in much overtime. There was a lot of things to be done, especially since he was going to leave in a few weeks. He had taken his laptop with him, but found himself staring at the screen at the same paragraph, unable to soak in any information. No, his mind was on one thing, or rather one person, and he kept glancing at his watch for when the hour was up because that meant she would be done with her yoga class and would come here to meet him.

Of course, there were other things on his mind. It was like a parasite in his brain, this unknown information between them. Unknown to her anyway. But how long should he wait before telling her? Before he left to go back to England? After the holidays?

His polar bear very much concurred with all of those ideas, so desperate for the bond to form soon. *I suppose it's not a bad idea.* He could enjoy the next few weeks with her, unhampered by obligations. They could just be ... them. Two people, together, with no cares in the world. Yes, that's what he should do.

Turning back to his work, he put all those thoughts away. The hour came and went, and he was so focused, he didn't realize she still wasn't here. A different emotion—worry—gripped him and turned his stomach sour. What if something had happened to her, like last week at the carnival?

He shut the lid of his laptop and stood, but to his relief, J.D. burst through the door, arm in arm with Dutchy Forrester as they laughed conspiratorially, their free hands holding shopping bags. Cam had met the fox shifter before at HQ as her mate, John Krieger, was also a ranger.

"Where were you?" he asked.

"I sent you a text message. Didn't you get it?" She tiptoed to kiss him on the cheek. "We decided to do some shopping."

"Oh? What did you get?"

Dutchy giggled and winked at J.D. "I'm gonna go pick up a coffee and muffin, then I have to meet John for an early dinner at my aunt's. See you next week, same time?"

"Of course, Dutch."

"Bye, guys." Dutchy waved as she sashayed toward the counter.

"Well?" He glanced down at the paper bags in her hand. "Did you get Christmas presents?"

"Kinda," she said, a twinkle in her eye. Lifting one of the bags up, he saw the familiar logo of Silk, Lace, and Whispers. "Maybe you can get to open an early present tonight."

He groaned inwardly. J.D. in her usual white cotton underwear—or nothing at all—was more than enough for him, but seeing her in lingerie would probably give him a heart attack.

She placed a hand on her cocked hip. "I'm just going to assume from your silence that you don't object?"

"You would assume correctly. Now let's go before I embarrass myself in front of all these people."

"Spenser, you have such a way with words, you know?"

Scooping up his things, he grabbed her hand and practically dragged her out of the coffee shop as she laughed all the way to the car.

They spent the rest of the day in bed as she modeled some of her new purchases. Of course, she had saved a few, promising him he could unwrap it on Christmas morning. He never thought he'd ever think this in his entire life, but he wished it was December twenty-fifth already.

Saturday afternoon turned to evening, and they ordered pizza for dinner and stayed up watching J.D.'s favorite Christmas movies on the big screen TV in the living room.

"You've never seen *White Christmas*?" she asked as they scrolled through the Movieflix menu of holiday movies.

"No, I haven't."

"Really?"

He rolled his eyes in an approximation of how she did it. "Asking me again won't make me have magically seen it."

She stuck her tongue out at him, then pressed on the TV remote. "All right, Scrooge, sit back, relax, and enjoy the splendor of Irving Berlin, Bing Crosby, Rosemary Clooney, and Danny Kaye."

Cam had to admit, it was a good movie and the music was excellent, though too sentimental for his tastes. But all he cared about was the fact that J.D. seemed to enjoy every moment of it, though he could guess she'd seen it a hundred times before.

"I was hoping we'd see snow by now," she said as the credits rolled. "But it looks like the weather reports can't be trusted."

"On average, a seven-day forecast can be reliable about eighty percent of the time," he said. "Go to ten-day, and it's about half."

"Or, it's waiting to come down at the right time."

"Right time? Weather isn't sentient."

"All right, can the nerdy talk, Dr. Spenser, before you turn me on." He could feel her roll her eyes. "I'm just saying ... maybe something magical will happen and it will start snowing, like in the movie." When he didn't say anything, she turned her head up at him. "What, you don't believe me?"

He harrumphed. "Woman, I've been around you long enough to know not to answer a loaded question like that."

A laugh burst from her mouth. "Oh, you. C'mere ..."

And so, there was no more talking or movies for the rest of the night. When he woke up the next day, Cam felt like he was on top of the world. His polar bear, too, was in a great mood, as if sensing that the bond was within their reach.

"If we're going to use up our energy like this," she groaned as he rolled off her after their first round of the day. "You're going to have to stock your fridge with more food."

He chuckled. "We still have pizza in the fridge. Let's heat it up, and then we can go to the supermarket."

They quickly dressed—her in his pajama top and him in the matching bottoms—and headed out to the kitchen. As J.D. took the boxes out of the fridge, his doorbell rang.

"Are you expecting anyone?"

He frowned. "No. But let me go get it." Who could be at his door this early? With an annoyed yank, he pulled the door open. "What in God's name—*babushka?*"

Natalia Dashokov had to crane her neck back to meet his gaze. "Aleksandr!" Her hands shot up, and he automatically bent down so she could kiss both his cheeks. "Surprise!"

This was some damned surprise, that was for sure. "Uh, good morning, *babushka,*" he managed to say. What was his grandmother doing here? "Where did you—" His stomach dropped, and his bear let out an annoyed grunt when he realized there was a second person with his grandmother.

"Surprise, Cam," Arabella Stepford-Pryde greeted, a blonde brow raised as she eyed his half-naked state. "Oh dear. I hope we haven't come at a bad time."

"What are *you* doing here?" he mustered in his coldest tone. He hadn't seen Arabella in five years. Well, it would be exactly five years on December twenty-fifth.

"*Bah*, Aleksandr," Natalia placed herself between them. "Please. I have traveled long and far. Won't you invite us in and make us some tea?"

His bear roared; its anger directed at Arabella. It seethed

at the thought of that vile woman in their den. "Why are you traveling with my grandmother?"

"Tut-tut, Cameron," Arabella cooed. "She invited me on the trip. Said that she hated these long flights and didn't want to be all alone."

When he gave his grandmother a stern warning gaze, Natalia flashed him an innocent look. "What?" She shrugged. "You know it is true. Please, *lyuba*."

"What's going on here?" came J.D.'s voice from behind. "Cam? Who's at the door?"

This was not happening. This was not happening. His perfect, idyllic dream was about to turn into a nightmare. *I should have told her!* "J.D.," he began as he turned around.

She was already behind him. "Is it those pesky mission— oh, hello," she said to Natalia and Arabella. "Can we help you?"

"Help us?" Arabella's nostrils flared, and her voice pitched higher. "And just who are you, and what are you doing here?"

J.D.'s expression turned stormy, and her arms crossed over her chest. "Excuse me? Who the hell do you think you are?"

"Lady Arabella Stepford-Pryde. Cam's fiancé," she sneered.

J.D. looked about ready to explode, but Cam put himself between the two women. "*Ex*-fiancée," he corrected. "We broke up years ago. And aren't you engaged to someone else now? To the football player?"

"Cam, please," Arabella laughed nervously. "Calling you my fiancé was a ... mere slip of the tongue. I'm just so used to saying it whenever I'm around you."

"Cameron Spenser, you've got some explaining to do," J.D. said, her teeth gnashing together.

Bugger. "I suppose I do." And possibly some groveling too.

"Aleksandr, who is this?" Natalia asked, a white brow raised so high it nearly reached her hairline.

Fuck me. If there is a god out there, strike me dead now. "Um, *babushka*, may I present, Ms. J.D. McNamara. J.D., this is my grandmother, Natalia Dashokov."

"Cam, where are your manners! I swear this country had turned you positively feral," Arabella admonished. "That's Her Royal Highness, Princess Natalia Dashokov."

J.D.'s jaw dropped. "P-princess?" She blinked several times. "She's a ... does that mean you're a ... prince?"

He massaged his temple. "No, no, I'm not a prince."

"Of course he isn't. Royal titles can't pass through the female line," Arabella stated as if that was a well-known fact, like the sky was blue or water was wet. "Cam is His Grace, the Duke of Westmoreland."

"Duke?" she cried. "*Duke?*"

"I prefer to be called by my professional title, the one *I* earned." And didn't inherit from a despicable, drunken wastrel.

"*Lyuba,*" his grandmother soothed. "It seems we have come at a bad time. Forgive me, for intruding on your ... ah ... morning. We will head back to our hotel and return later."

"*Babushka,* no." He hated cliches, but he was stuck between a rock and hard place. And looking at his grandmother's sweet, understanding expression and J.D.'s nearly explosive one, he couldn't find a better metaphor. "Don't go."

"That's right," J.D. said through gritted teeth. "Don't trouble yourself. I'll be the one leaving." And with that, she turned on her heel and marched back into the apartment.

"Bloody hell." A throbbing headache began to form between his eyebrows.

"*Lyuba*, who was that lady?"

Arabella snorted. "If you could call her that."

He sent his former fiancé a warning glare, then turned to his grandmother. "That was ... my surprise to you," he said, switching to Russian for privacy.

"Surprise? I don't understand."

"J.D. is my mate," he stated. "My fated mate."

Natalia's white brows furrowed. "Your ... oh!" Her frail, wrinkled fingers gripped his forearms. "That is wonderful news! Oh! Does that mean ... does she know that you must return to Europe?"

"Yes, *babushka*. And she is ... willing to make things work between us." Well, she *was* anyway.

"Oh, my dear ... you do not know how happy this—" She stopped short, then her gaze flickered to Arabella. "Oh, forgive me! The trouble this must be causing. I only thought that perhaps since Arabella recently broke up with her fiancé that you and her...."

It all made sense now. His grandmother had adored Arabella, mostly because his former fiancé hid her true, viperous nature from her. Natalia must have thought that Cam's distaste for the holiday when they broke up meant he still carried a torch for her, and bringing her along was a misguided plot to get them back together.

"Pardon me," Arabella interrupted, obviously sensing

they were talking about her. "But, Cam, now that your *guest* is leaving, perhaps you could invite us in?"

When hell froze over. His polar bear agreed with a chuff, crossing its front paws over its chest. He would have to take the direct approach. "I don't think it's a good idea. I'd ask my grandmother to stay, but you on the other hand—"

"But, Cam—"

"I said *no*," he roared, letting his bear come to the surface close enough for his eyes to take on a glow and his front incisors to briefly pop out.

Her mouth quickly shut, and her body went rigid. *Good.* That was one way to shut her up and keep her away, to let out that part of him she had abhorred so much. He would never forget or forgive her for the words he'd overheard.

You know what they say about athletes, she had tittered to her friend. *They're animals in bed. And since I'll soon have an animal for a husband, why not have my cake and eat it too?*

Arabella should have done more research on *animals*, because she had no idea he could hear her six feet away, even in a crowded ballroom at a Christmas party.

"Arabella," Natalia began, using her most regal tone. "You've been such a dear to me during our travels. But, would you be ever so kind as to give my grandson and me a few minutes of privacy? Please?" Anyone who knew the princess knew that was *not* a request.

Arabella looked like she was about to explode, but, her good breeding won out. She took in a sharp breath and curtsied. "Of course, Your Highness. I shall wait in the limo." Keeping her eyes cast low, she scurried to the elevator.

When they were finally alone, Natalia put a hand on his arm. "*Lyuba*, I have made trouble for you." His grandmother's penitent tone made his heart clench. "You must let me make things right."

"It's fine, *babushka*. I'll fix it."

"Are you sure? You know I can always make things better."

"You do, *babushka*, you always do." Putting an arm around her, he led her inside. "But this is something I must do myself."

"I understand, and I have complete faith that you and your mate will reconcile and all will be well." She waggled her eyebrows at him. "And perhaps the great-grand babies—"

"*Babushka*," he groaned. "Please. One step at a time." He guided her to the couch. "What are you doing here, by the way? Don't get me wrong, I'm so glad to see you after all these months. But you didn't have to come all the way here. I will keep my word and fly out in January. I was just hoping to settle things with J.D. and have her come to London to meet you."

"Ah, yes!" Her face lit up and her hands clapped together. "I was so desperate to see you, and then an invitation arrived, and I knew it was meant to be that I come here."

"Invitation? What invitation?"

"Your dear cousin is coming to Blackstone for the holidays. There will be a grand ball and everything to welcome him and his family."

He let out a blue streak in Russian that would have made his grandfather and ancestors proud.

"Aleksandr!"

"Sorry, *babushka*." *I knew I should have explained it to J.D.,* he thought to himself. There was just so much information, and he knew it would overwhelm her. "If you wait a moment, I'll go talk to J.D. first. Then we can sit down and have tea, all right? Do you need anything?"

"No, *lyuba*, I am fine here."

"All right. I'll try not to be too long."

After making sure his grandmother was comfortable, he went off in the direction of his bedroom. "J.D.?" he called as he padded inside. "Love, are you in here?" Her scent was still in the air, so she had been here last, but there was no sign of her. Her clothes that had been on the dresser, however, were gone, and the window next to it was left wide open.

He slapped his forehead. She had shifted and left through the window.

His polar bear roared in anger, its sharp claws slashing at him.

Ow, stop it! And by the way, this is your fault, you know.

It cocked its head at him as if to say, *How?*

Things wouldn't have gone cock-up if you had let me tell her about grandmother and— "Oh bloody fucking hell."

He wasn't going to argue with a polar bear. *All right, I'm going to fix this.*

First, he was going to take care of his grandmother, then he was going to hunt J.D. down. He knew he was wrong to have kept the truth from her for this long, but she didn't have to fucking leap off a building to get away from him. He was in this for the long haul, and he could only hope she would be too.

Chapter 11

Escaping Cam's penthouse took a lot of trouble and effort, but it was well worth it. After she stormed back into the bedroom, she realized that there was no way she could get out without having to face Cam or his "guests."

But she wasn't out of options, and in one impulsive decision, she decided to chuck her clothes and wallet out the window, then shift into her cat form, crawling down using the drain pipe outside the building. From there, it was easy enough to walk out to the main road and flag down a passing cab.

"Five twenty-two, Magnolia Drive," she rattled off to the driver as she slipped into the back seat. "And step on it."

She'd been so furious that she couldn't stand to be in the same space as that ... that liar. Her cat, on the other hand, directed it at that snooty bitch trying to lay claim of their mate.

He's not even worth it, she told her cat. *We should just forget about him.* "Ugh." It was too early to be arguing with

149

her animal. She covered her eyes with her hand as an ache bloomed in her chest at Cam's betrayal. *Mates suck ass.* She wished she'd never laid eyes on Dr. Cameron Spenser, Duke of Whatever-he-was.

Her cat let out a protesting *re-eowrl. Coward,* it seemed to say.

"He's the coward," she mumbled so the driver couldn't hear her. "And a fucking liar."

The cab slowed down, and she saw her house up ahead. "Third one on the right," she told the driver. "Thanks," she said when he stopped in front of her house, then handed him a bill. "And keep the change."

She hopped out of the cab, barefoot and only wearing her jeans and shirt, and made her way to the house. When she was about halfway there, she realized something.

"Shit! Fuck, fuck, shit!" Her house keys were back at Cam's along with her phone. There was no way she was getting inside now, and her truck was still at the garage. "Fffuuuuuuck me." *This was all Cam's fault.*

How, her cat seemed to ask as it tilted its head to the side.

"I ... I don't know, just leave me alone." Trudging to the porch steps, she sat down, then buried her face in her hands.

This last week ... she'd never felt this way before, about anyone. Never had such a fun time with someone, in and out of bed.

But he was still a liar. He didn't tell her about his grandmother being a princess or about being a duke himself, nor had he mentioned anything about previously being engaged.

Just thinking of that woman had her blood boiling,

especially with the way she looked down her nose at her. Like she wasn't even fit to kiss Cam's shoes.

J.D. honestly thought she'd gotten over that high school queen bee shit. That she was more than just the tomboy mechanic's daughter who didn't know how to put on lipstick or match her shoes with her belt.

The ache in her chest grew, thinking about Cam and that woman. They must have made a striking couple—him, so handsome and tall, her, so elegant and gorgeous and perfect. All that they'd shared together. Wrapped up in bed together. How he must have loved her enough to ask her to marry him.

Tears sprung to her eyes. "Great," she sniffed. And now she was crying over him. How could this day possibly get any worse?

"J.D., I ... hey, are you okay?" a familiar voice asked.

Damn it! She should have known better than to ask. In her head, she looked up at the sky, spread her arms apart, and screamed, *really?*

"J.D.?"

Wiping her eyes with her shirt sleeve, she took a calming breath and looked up at Roy Jorrell. "Hey, Roy," she greeted, pasting a smile on her face. "Wow, I am just bumping into you everywhere, aren't I? Are you driving past my house checking if I'm home?" she joked.

"I was just in the neighborhood," he said sheepishly. "Thought I'd drop by to check on you. You know. After the carnival and everything."

"Oh, right."

"I was calling you all week," he said. "But you weren't picking up."

"Been super busy. Holidays, you know?"

"Whoa!" Roy's eyes went wide as he glanced behind her. "What happened there?"

"What happened—Aww, fuck me with a dirty cactus!" she cursed when she turned her head and followed Roy's gaze. Someone had spray-painted "Bitch Whore" all over her door in red paint. "Motherfucking twunt pipers! I'm going to kill whoever did this."

"Who do you think could have done this?" Roy asked. "Is it a prank?"

"I ... I don't know." Her shoulders sank. God, what a mess. All she wanted to do was have a sinkhole open up and swallow her whole.

"Why don't we go inside?" he suggested. "I can make you some coffee or tea."

"We can't," she said. "I don't have my keys."

"You don't?"

"Yeah, I, uh, left them at Cam's."

"Do you need to call him to get them back?"

"Left my phone there too."

His brows furrowed. "J.D., where is he? And why are you here all alone and barefoot?"

She pursed her lips together, wanting to confide into someone what an asshole her mate was. It was tempting, and she knew Roy would have a sympathetic ear. "Listen, Roy, could you do me a favor?"

"Anything."

"Could you, uh, drive me to Rosie's on Main Street? My friend works there, and he can get me sorted." Gabriel had a copy of her house key, and she could at least get started from there.

"Of course. Come, my lady." He gestured to his truck. "My chariot awaits."

Oh, brother. But it wasn't like she had much choice. So, she stood up and followed him. He opened the passenger side door for her, but before she could hop in, a familiar Range Rover drove up to them, then turned into her driveway.

Crap! She wanted to hop into the truck and tell Roy to floor it, but her damned cat wouldn't let her. In fact, it yowled and hissed and clawed at her insides, and she only had a foot up on the jacked-up Sierra's running board. *Get in, dummy,* she told her body. But it wouldn't budge.

A pissed-off looking Cam hopped out of the Range Rover and marched straight toward her and Roy. His expression only got angrier and angrier as he came closer. "Where do you think you're going with *my* mate?" If looks could kill, Roy would have died on the spot.

"Somewhere she'll be safe," Roy shot back.

"And what are you implying? That she's not safe with me?"

"Cam!" she warned. "Stop it. You have no right to be here."

"No right?" he asked incredulously. "May I remind you, you were the one who snuck out of a window."

"And whose fault was that?" she shot back. "Roy, can we go now? I need to get my keys from Gabriel."

"I have your keys," he said, fishing them out of his pocket and dangling them in front of her. "Now get away from this penis extension vehicle so we can go inside and have a civilized conversation."

Roy's face turned red. "Who do you think you are, you asshole!"

Cam stretched up to full height, which was about half a foot taller than Roy, then crossed his arms over his chest. "Want to try me?"

"For fuck's sake, put your dicks away." J.D. slapped a hand on her forehead. With a long sigh, she turned to Roy. "Listen, Roy, thanks so much, but I can take it from here."

"But he's—"

"It's all right," she assured him. "He has my keys, and I can get into my house." She didn't want to talk to Cam, but it was much easier to get her keys from him than to have to go all the way to Gabriel's. He would ask her questions, and Damon would get involved, and the whole thing would be a big fucking mess. "Sorry to have bothered you."

"Not a bother at all." He glared at Cam, who sent him a seething look. "Bye, J.D.." Hopping into his truck, he sped away with a final deafening roar of his engine.

"Wanker," Cam spat. "What the hell was he doing here?"

She folded her arms over her chest. "I thought you didn't get jealous?" When he didn't answer, she rolled her eyes. "Just give me my keys."

"Not until you sit down and talk to me."

"I don't want to talk to a liar like you. Now, give. Me. My. Keys."

"I wasn't lying," he pointed out. "I thought you said I can fill in the details later? And not to 'sweat the small stuff'?"

"Those were *very* big details to leave out!" she screamed back.

"Fine." He grabbed her hand and put the keys in her palm. "Here. Take them. But I'm not the only one lying here."

"What?" she snarled at him. "I have never lied to you, Dr. Duke Cameron Aleksandr, whatever your name is!"

"Oh yeah?" His blue-violet eyes blazed. "What about when you told me that nothing I could say could make you not want me?"

The true, genuine hurt in his eyes made her heart clench. *Oh God.*

He was right.

She had promised him. Remembering the anxiety in his eyes, she recalled how much courage it took to even open up to her, a virtual stranger at that point. But he did it because he wanted to be with her.

I can't quite imagine my life without you.

She blinked as the air rushed back into her lungs. "Cam!"

He was already climbing into his vehicle. "Wait!" She dashed after him, tugging at the back of his jacket, forcing him to turn around. "Cam, you're right, please, I'm sorry! I shouldn't have—"

Arms wrapped around her as his mouth captured hers in a hot, soulful kiss. It took her a second, but she responded back, pouring every emotion she had into kissing him back, arching her body into his in a desperate attempt to get as close to him as possible.

"J.D.," he breathed against her mouth. "I tried to tell you. I was going to. But I was swept away. This week ... it's been the best of my life."

"Me too," she confessed. "And I'm sorry, too, for walking out like that. For not hearing you out. I was just so stunned and ... and jealous."

"Jealous?"

"Yeah. Of ... her." She winced. But even now, the ugly

green monster inside of her was rearing its head inside her. "That you and her—"

"Oh, dear God. J.D., love, no." He kissed her again. "That's in the past. And even then, I wasn't really ..." He took a deep breath. "Can we go inside, please? And talk? I promise I'll tell you everything. It might take a while, but I promise you'll know everything."

"All right," she said. "Let's go inside." She was about to escort him to the front door but remembered the graffiti there. Not wanting to deal with that yet or explain it, she tugged him toward the back door instead. "On second thought, we should go to the kitchen. I'll make coffee."

"Here you go." J.D. handed Cam a mug of fresh, hot coffee, then sat beside him at her kitchen table.

"Thank you." He accepted it from her, then took a sip before placing it on top of the table. His hands wrapped around the cup. "I don't know where to begin."

She gnawed her lip with her teeth. "How about with your grandmother?" Inside, she winced. She'd acted so rude that morning to the sweet old lady who'd practically raised Cam.

"Yes. Princess Natalia of Zaratena. It was a small country in the Baltic region."

"Was?"

"Yeah. There was a revolution a few decades ago when my grandmother was a teenager. The people rose up and rebelled against my great-grandfather, the king, and the monarchy was overthrown. Not that it mattered because without a strong leader, Zaratena was eventually swallowed up by its neighboring countries."

"And your grandmother ... she escaped?"

"Yes."

"What about the rest of her family?"

"They ... were not all as lucky. The king, queen, and the crown prince and his family all perished. She had one older brother who was living abroad at the time, in Scandinavia. Grandmother was taken away by their most loyal servants and spirited to Russia where she lived in exile with distant relatives. When she was eighteen, she met my grandfather, Igor Dashokov. He was ... not a very nice person.

"The Dashokovs were a well-known polar bear shifter crime family. Igor's father started as a petty thief on the streets of St. Petersburg, but he grew his gang into a true criminal organization. When Igor took over, he wanted to go legitimate, and so he built upon his father's empire, getting into almost every kind of business there was. Oil. Gold. Energy. Agriculture. Over here, you've probably never heard of his name or his company, MedvedDaz, but there, it's a kind of a big deal. But, despite his wealth and power, Igor was hated by the elite of Russia. The members of the high society couldn't see past his criminal origins or his low birth. Even with all the money in the world, there was one thing he couldn't buy: respect and approval."

He paused, then took a long sip of the coffee. "He married my grandmother so he could elevate himself. The rest of the family objected, but he was determined to have his princess and sire well-bred, strong polar bear sons to continue the line. He promised—no, he pledged an oath to his brothers —that he would produce an heir to take over the business when he was gone. It was the only way they allowed the marriage and the legitimizing of their businesses.

"Unfortunately, their union only produced a daughter. My mother. But that didn't stop him, so he married her off to someone who could expand his business's reach across Europe and get his foot in the door in places where he'd normally be snubbed."

She gasped. "Your parents ... their marriage was arranged?"

"In a way, yes. My father's father, the old duke, was up to his eyeballs in debt. But he had a title and connections, and Igor knew *no one* would ever close their doors on a duke and the grandson of royalty."

"So you ... that's why you have to go back? To take over your grandfather's business? Because he literally promised you away even before you were born?"

"Yes."

There was a sadness there, in his eyes. "You don't want to go."

"I ... no."

"Because you love your work," she said in a quiet voice. "You'd rather be in the bogs, digging up birds' nests and literal shit than living the high life in Europe."

A smile curled up at the corner of her mouth. "Among other things."

"Then don't go," she said. "Stay here." *With me*, she added silently.

"It's not just a promise," he said. "It's a blood oath. It cannot be broken. If I don't go, then the remaining Dashokovs —my uncles and cousins—will consider the oath broken. And ... they'll want repayment."

"Repayment?"

"Yes. In the form of my grandmother's life."

"What!" She shot to her feet. "They would ... how ... no, they couldn't ..."

He nodded. "You don't know my family. They take honor seriously. So, you see, that's what I was afraid to tell you. I didn't want you to get involved in all that. If you want to be with me, then you'll have to live in Russia. Be my mate, bear my children. And I think ... you would hate it."

"You don't know that, Cam."

"You wouldn't have this." He gestured around him. "Or your friends. Your garage. You'd have to leave Blackstone eventually. I couldn't do that to you."

"You're right. I wouldn't have all this." She reached over and took his hands in hers. "But I'd have you."

Hope flared in his eyes. "J.D., think about what you're saying."

"I am." Standing up, she circled around to his side, then planted herself in his lap. "I told you, we would work it out. And I'm not backing down or bowing out just because you were born into a family of psychos."

"You won't?"

"Nuh-uh." And she wasn't about to let some Russian gangsters make a sweet old lady sleep with the fishes. "And all this?" She glanced around. "It would mean nothing if I can't be with you."

"God ... J.D. ..." His hands clamped around the back of her head and pulled her in for a long, hard, deep kiss. "I'll make you happy. I promise. Anything and everything you want; I'll give it to you. I'll buy you a slew of garages across the continent."

She pulled him to her, laying his head on her shoulder. "But what about you? What about your happiness? Your work ... science ..."

"It doesn't matter," he said. "As long as my grandmother is safe and I have you."

But it did matter. It mattered to *her*. Somehow, she would find a way so he, too, could have everything he wanted. "So, that's it? That's all?"

"Well, two more things I supposed." Pulling away from her, he straightened his glasses, which had gone askew. "First, Arabella."

"Ugh." Her cat snarled. "Do we *have* to talk about her?"

"Unfortunately, yes. Because I want you to know, she means nothing to me. We broke up five years ago because she cheated on me."

"Oh. I'm so sorry, Cam." And now she wanted to hurt that heifer even more. Slice her to ribbons and put her head on a stick. Then take the head off and have her cat play with it like a ball of yarn. Her animal purred, relishing the thought.

"It's fine, really. When it all ended, I was mostly relieved. I suppose I cared about her in a way, but she only wanted me for my title and wealth. Our fathers were friends, and they very much encouraged the match."

Emotion flickered in his eyes at the mention of his father, but that was a sensitive topic they could table for now. "So, what was she doing here?"

"It was my grandmother's idea. She was in favor of the match too. After all, Arabella was the daughter of an earl, well-bred, cultured, beautiful, and had all the right connections."

Her lips pursed. "Please go on and tell me more about your perfect ex."

He kissed her nose. "Now, now, love. She may have had all those things, but she's not worth your pinky finger. Natalia only saw the good side of her."

"But if she cheated on you, why would your grandmother bring her here?" She waited for an answer, but Cam's silence said it all. "She didn't know, did she? You didn't tell her Arabella cheated on you?"

He shrugged. "It didn't matter. If anyone asked, Arabella said it just didn't work out, and I didn't contradict her. Then she made it official with her football star a few months later. What's the use of sullying her reputation when I didn't really care much for her anyway? Besides, it would break my grandmother's heart."

She stared at him, all agog. Any other man in his position would have reveled in the fact that Arabella had been the one caught with someone else. Claimed the moral high ground and painted her as a cheating whore.

But this was Cam. Honorable. Respectful. Unselfish. Of course he would protect Arabella's reputation, even though she hurt him. "You're a better person than I am," she said with a shake of her head.

"Don't worry, my grandmother promised she'll send Arabella home. We'll never have to see her again."

That gave her some sense of relief, and her cat didn't feel like scratching him up anymore ... not too much anyway. "Now, the third, and hopefully final thing?"

"Ah, yes." He cleared his throat. "The reason why my grandmother's here in the first place. There's this thing ..."

"Thing?"

"A party. Ball, really. On Christmas Eve. To welcome my cousin who's coming for a visit."

"Cousin? You have a cousin?"

"Second cousin. Natalia's one living older brother had a daughter, who in turn had a son. You might have heard of him, but you definitely know his wife, formerly known as Sybil Lennox."

"Sybil ... as in, Queen Sybil?" Oh, she'd heard about his mate all right. "*Jesus Jehoshaphat Christ*, the dragon king is your cousin?"

"Second cousin," he reminded her. "We're related through the human sides of our family tree."

Her mind was reeling. No, scratch that—it spun like she was doing an impression of the little girl from *The Exorcist*. *Welcome to the family,* Jason Lennox had said. Welcome indeed.

"So, my grandmother would very much like for us to be, uh, presented to them at the ball. And basically, to everyone and the world to cement your status as my mate."

Her mind blanked. Someone once told her that she could swear in a way that would make a sailor blush, but somehow, she couldn't come up with anything at this moment. Like her brain just said, *nope, I'm out of here,* then walked out the door and slammed it behind her.

"J.D.? Are you all right?"

"Huh?" She blinked. "Um. Yeah."

"This is a lot, I know. Which is why I was so afraid to tell you all this. This last week with you has been the best in my life. I just wanted more of it. More time to spend with you. As *me*. Not a future oligarch, grandson of a princess, or titled aristocrat. Just me. *Cam*."

Her heart clenched at the sincerity in his voice and the depth of real emotion in his face. "And that's who I want."

His arms came around her. "J.D. ..."

She melted into him and met his mouth halfway. *Oh, Cam.* This whole thing was huge. No, it was enormous and so gigantic that it could swallow her whole until there was nothing left. Her stomach churned. But, feeling Cam's lips on hers, being in his arms, she could ignore those fears. "All right," she murmured against his mouth.

"All ... right?"

"I mean ... yes. I'll come to the ball and do whatever you need me to do. To ... save your grandmother and for us to be together."

Relief crossed his face. "J.D., I promise you, you won't regret this."

"But you'll have to give me time too," she said. "And some patience."

"Of course, you'll have whatever you need." His hands gripped her arms. "This is just a formality. Think of it like going to the prom, so everyone knows we're together."

She snorted. "I never went to prom."

"Why not?"

"No one ever asked." And Damon and Gabriel already had dates, so it wasn't like she could go stag with them. "Didn't want to go anyway. My old man and I spent it watching horror movies. Anyway, so this is just a Christmas party? To meet your family and let them know we're going steady?"

"Yes. It would mean so much to my grandmother."

She took a very deep breath. "All right. I suppose

everything will be fine. It's Sybil, and she's cool. We can have my friends there, right?"

"Of course," he said. "Whatever you want. Invite whomever you want."

"I suppose I'll have to put on a dress."

"Uh ..."

She crossed her arms over her chest. "This is the second time I'll be putting on a fancy dress this year, Spenser. One's usually my limit, but ... you're so lucky that you've got a cute smile and a nice ass."

The atmosphere in the kitchen lightened significantly, and a smile spread across his face. "I don't deserve you, J.D."

"Well, I'm what you got." She kissed his nose. "So ... your grandmother. She'll be in Blackstone until the ball?"

"Yes. And she's so eager to meet you, so I've set up afternoon tea with her tomorrow at three."'

"T-tomorrow?" she gulped. "Uh, I mean, that's great."

"Don't be nervous, love," he assured her. "She'll adore you. I promise, everything will go splendidly."

When she thought of Cam's grandmother, she envisioned a sweet old lady who lived in a cottage in the English countryside, tending her garden and spoiling her two corgis. Not a princess who was also related to a dragon. "All right." She blew out a breath. "Three o'clock it is." God, the thought was making her temple throb and her stomach flip-flop.

It's worth it, she told herself. Especially now, as she saw Cam's handsome face light up with happiness. *This is going to work out.*

Spending time with Cam, getting to know him this past week and seeing who he really is—the person that he was, not everything else that came with him—she knew there would be no one else for her. Hell, he was willing to like Christmas for her, doing all those Christmassy things with her this week, for fuck's sake. The least she could do was try to fit into his world. She was going to do her goddamn best to make it work.

Because, frankly, she couldn't quite live without him either.

Chapter 12

Since he knew his departure would be inevitable, Cam set up a meeting with Damon the very next day to let him know what was going on.

As he sat behind his oak desk, Damon shook his head. "I'm mighty disappointed you won't be staying, Cam."

"The contract was until the end of the year," he reminded the chief. "You always knew I would be leaving."

"Yeah, but with J.D. being your mate, I was kinda hoping you'd stay. We could use someone like you, not just as a ranger, but someone with your scientific knowledge."

That caught him by surprise. "Really?"

"Yeah." Damon folded his hands together on top of the desk, but when their eyes met, the chief quickly retracted them.

Bollocks. Of course, Damon remembered what happened on top of this very desk. And so did Cam, which was why he shifted uncomfortably in his seat. "Er, you were saying, Chief?"

Dark brows slashed together, and Damon cleared his

throat. "Yeah. We never really had a full-time scientist on the team. Sure, we hired out for anything we needed, but no one was really interested in any long-term study. The reports and papers you wrote, I read them all, and I have to say, it's all top-notch stuff."

"You ... read them all?"

"Well, read them, but not necessarily understood every word." He smirked. "But, your recommendations for the preservation of the wildlife and flora, your observations about our operations, and even your tracking of the migratory species passing through have been valuable in helping me make decisions, as well as reporting back to Lennox. They've even approved more funding to help preserve more of the mountain."

His work had always been academic and research-driven, but he'd never thought it could lead to practical results he'd be able to see with his own eyes. *Well, not quite.* His stomach dropped as he remembered that he wasn't going to be around to see the fruits of his labors. No, a few months from now, he'd be stuck in boardrooms and glass offices and boring business dinners.

"Anyway," Damon continued as he stood up. "We're really lucky to have had you with us, Cam." He held out a hand. "Good luck."

"Thank you, Chief. And thank you for allowing me to leave early today to see my grandmother." He took the offered hand and shook it. "By the way, there's an event on Christmas Eve I wanted to speak to you about." He gave Damon a quick rundown about the ball at Blackstone Castle. "It would mean a lot to J.D.—us, I mean—if you and Anna Victoria could come. She's invited everyone, actually."

"Then I'll probably hear it from Anna Victoria myself. And of course, we'll be there." The chief's expression changed. "And Cam, I know I don't have to say this, but ... you'll take care of her, right?" His eyes briefly glowed with the presence of his Kodiak.

His polar bear's temper flared for a second, huffing at the idea that they couldn't take care of their mate, but Cam pushed it away. "Of course. You have nothing to worry about. She'll want for nothing." Though he himself only used his inheritance from Igor sparingly, J.D. would have unlimited access to his wealth to do with as she pleased.

"I'm not talking about money," he said. "But that's all I'll say about it since your relationship is none of my business."

Goddamn right it wasn't. "Thank you, Chief. I shall see you around and at the ball."

After picking up his things, he went to the locker room to change into a smart casual outfit consisting of dark trousers, a dress shirt, sweater, a jacket, plus leather shoes. This was afternoon tea with the princess, after all, and he was expected to act and dress accordingly.

Of course, that was information he should have relayed to J.D. this morning.

He'd never really paid much attention to what clothes his mate put on—as he was usually far too busy taking them off her. But when he walked into the hotel lobby and saw her dressed in a red flannel shirt, jeans, boots, and her customary trucker cup, he realized his mistake.

"Hey, Cam," she greeted as she got on her tiptoes to kiss him on the cheek. "Everything went okay with Damon?" He had told her about his meeting with the chief this afternoon.

"Yeah." He wondered what to tell her about her outfit

without insulting her. Even with his lack of experience with women, he was very sure insulting their clothing wasn't the best way to start a conversation.

"Cam?" She cocked her head to the side. "What's wrong now?"

"Er ..." He gritted his teeth. This was his fault for not warning her, so he was going to take responsibility should Natalia say anything about it. "Nothing, love."

She chuckled. "And I thought I was nervous. So, are we going to meet your grandmother at the restaurant?"

"No, we're having tea up in her private suite. I—what's that?" He nodded at the large paper bag in her hand.

"Oh! I wanted to give your grandma a gift," she began. "I couldn't decide exactly what, since what do you get a princess? But I went to the gift shop anyway and got some Blackstone souvenirs." Reaching in, she took out a small object. It looked to be a plaster model of the mountains and Welcome to Blackstone was painted on a banner in the front. "Jan down at the gift shop said these magnets were her best sellers. Your grandmother can put them on her fridge."

Cam highly doubted Natalia had ever seen the fridge in any of her homes, nor even knew where they would be located. "Uh ... that's lovely, J.D. A sweet gesture."

"I got her a snow globe, a cap, T-shirt, and a cute stuffed cat. No polar bears, unfortunately, but Jan said she can stock those up before New Year."

"Excellent." He glanced at his watch. "We should get going. Natalia is very punctual and expects everyone to be as well." He led her toward the elevators and hit the floor for the presidential suite.

The elevator reached its destination, and they stepped

out. J.D. let out a whistle as they stepped into the foyer. "Wow. I've been to this hotel a couple times, but I've never been up here. This sure is nice."

They walked to the single door, where two burly men in dark suits stood, unmoving. Cam recognized them as two of Natalia's bodyguards, a bear shifter who was an ex-Russian Armed Forces soldier, and a former Ghurka tiger shifter. Neither one of them moved as they already knew Cam, though their gazes flickered over J.D. suspiciously. He sent them a warning glare and tucked her hand into the crook of his arm. Before he could say anything, the door opened.

"Ah, Your Grace." The man in the charcoal gray suit bowed deeply. "Welcome. It's lovely to see you again."

"Hello, Orson," he greeted Natalia's ever-present, ever-loyal butler as he handed him his jacket. "This is Ms. J.D. McNamara."

"Ms. McNamara." He bowed his head. "It's a pleasure to meet you."

"Orson is my grandmother's butler," Cam explained.

"Butler?" J.D. raised a brow. "Like, Alfred in *Batman*? You guys really exist?"

Decades of training and serving under his grandparents had perfected Orson's poker face. "Yes, miss." His gaze flickered to her hat, and he held out his hands. "May I?"

"Oh, sure." J.D. grabbed both his hands and shook them vigorously. "Nice to meet ya."

And it looked like Orson's training was to be tested today, as the butler let out a sputtering sound before he clamped his lips shut. To his credit, he managed to compose himself as soon as J.D. let go. "May I take your hat?"

"My hat?"

Cam placed a hand on her shoulder. "It's all right, J.D., he's just going to put it in the closet while we have tea."

"Oh, sure." She handed him her hat. "Don't lose that now, okay, buddy? That was my dad's."

"I shall guard it with my life," he said. "Now, if you both could follow me, please." Orson led them into the entryway and out to the massive, elegantly-decorated living room. "His Grace and Ms. McNamara have arrived, ma'am," Orson announced.

"Welcome," Natalia greeted. She was dressed in a crisp yellow skirt suit, matching hat, shoes and white gloves, and sat in one of the plush armchairs. "*Lyuba*, it is lovely to see you."

They walked over to her, and he bent down to kiss her cheek. "*Babushka,* you look well. Your Highness, may I present, Ms. J.D. McNamara." He ushered her forward. "My mate."

"It's nice to meet you, princess. Er, Highness?" J.D. laughed nervously. "Sorry. I'm not sure—"

"Ma'am is fine," Cam said. "After the first time you addressed her as Your Highness."

"Oh, gotcha." She winked at him, then turned to Natalia. "Your Highness. Nice to meet you, ma'am."

Natalia's lips curved up slowly, and she sent an amused look at Cam. "Likewise." She motioned to the couch diagonally opposite from where she sat. "Please, have a seat."

"Cam didn't tell me I was supposed to dress up fancy, sorry about that, Highness—er, ma'am," she said as she smoothed a hand down her jeans. "At least I changed into my clean clothes," she chortled. "Wouldn't want to mess up this white couch by getting grease stains all over it."

"It's entirely my fault, *babushka*," he quickly said to Natalia. "Please forgive me."

"Bah." She waved a hand away. "It is fine. We are just ... friends having tea, are we not?" she said to J.D.

"Yeah, that's what I thought. Like, going out for coffee, right?" She chortled. "Oh! By the way ..." She handed the paper bag to Natalia. "Here. I got these for you."

A white brow rose. "For me?"

"Yeah. They're Blackstone souvenirs. I wasn't sure if you'd have time to go shopping, so I got you a bit of everything just in case."

Ever gracious, Natalia accepted the bag. "How kind of you. May I?"

"Go ahead."

Natalia reached into the bag and took out the contents. "Oh ... my ..." The first thing she took out was a camouflage T-shirt that said "I love Blackstone" with a heart symbol instead of the word love. It came with a matching trucker cap. There were more fridge magnets, stuffed toy cat, and a keychain. "Er ... thank you so much, my dear, you are so thoughtful."

If the image of his grandmother wearing the ridiculous hat and shirt hadn't made him smile inwardly, he would have groaned in embarrassment. "Er, yes, why don't we let Orson take those away." *Far, far away.*

Natalia stuffed everything back into the bag, and Orson rushed over to take it from her. "I'll keep this one here, though," she said, placing the stuffed cat on her lap.

The beaming look on J.D.'s face made his heart clench. It was obvious she had taken that as a sign of Natalia's approval, and Cam sighed with relief.

Natalia nodded at Orson when he reappeared. "Orson, please have the staff begin the tea service."

"Right away, ma'am."

She turned to J.D. and Cam. "Now, you two are mates, correct? And you are a shifter? Tell me, how did you know my Aleksandr was your mate? Was it when you met? What happened?"

"Well, that's one hell of a—uh, heckuva story," J.D. said, snorting. "You see, I was stealing some candy from—"

"J.D., she doesn't need to know all the details of our meet-cute." He emphasized the last word, to remind her of that conversation they had after said meet-cute.

"Our meet—oh. Right." She winked at him not-so-inconspicuously. "Ma'am, I didn't know you knew about mates. You're human, correct?"

"Oh, yes. And of course I do." She clapped her hands together. "I was recently informed of the existence of mates. As you know, Aleksandr's dear cousin, King Aleksei, met his own fated mate in Queen Sybil. The strength of their union is renowned. Such a happy couple, and they produced the most adorable prince." Her expression brightened. "Oh my, and it *must* be fate that my Aleksandr should find his own mate here as well. Had I known, I wouldn't have objected to him coming to Blackstone so much. And I can't believe it took you so long to meet." She tsked. "All this time wasted."

"It was only a few months, *babushka*."

"When you have as little time left as I, a few months is a lifetime. If you had met her the moment you stepped off the plane, she might already be breeding—".

"*Babushka,*" he warned, as gently as he could.

Thank goodness Orson, his under butler, and the maid

arrived with the tea service. They set down cups, a teapot, cream, and a tiered tray filled with various savories and sweets, plus plates of scones and pots of jam and clotted cream.

"Wow," J.D. exclaimed. "Great spread. I thought we were just drinking tea," she snorted. "I even practiced lifting my pinkie and everything." And to show them, she took a teacup and saucer, put it to her lips, her pinkie lifting into an exaggerated position. The clattering sound of the cup hitting the saucer when she put it down made Natalia start, her hand going to her chest.

"Uh, J.D., love," he said gently, taking his grandmother's delicate, hundred-year-old china away from J.D. "It's only a myth that that's how you drink tea. You don't have to do that." *Dear Lord, please don't*, he added silently.

"Oh. Sorry," she said sheepishly at Natalia.

Cam cleared his throat. "May I pour you some tea, *babushka?*"

The rest of the tea proceeded without much incident. Cam tried his best to steer the conversation away from J.D., so she wouldn't feel like she was being interrogated or pressured with great-grandchildren talk. He asked Natalia about her travels and how she spent the last few months, how her friends were as such, and what the latest gossip was back in England. When J.D. started fidgeting and stirring her spoon in her teacup with a loud clanging sound, he gently placed his hand on top of hers to make her stop. Silently, she withdrew her hand and leaned back on the couch.

"So," Natalia began, turning to J.D. "Aleksandr has told you about the ball at Blackstone Castle, yes?"

"Uh, kinda, yeah."

"I am so looking forward to it, and seeing my grand-nephew again," Natalia continued. "Cam and I have not seen him or his queen since the wedding. By the way, are you acquainted with Queen Sybil?"

"Oh yeah. I saved her when she got drunk at a party, and now her father lets me chop down a tree in his mountains for Christmas."

Natalia's brows furrowed. "Chop down a—"

"What she means is," Cam interrupted, squeezing J.D.'s knee. "She saved Her Majesty's life when they were young. The Blackstone Dragon was so thankful that he gave J.D. a reward."

"You saved her ..." Natalia's eyes widened. "It really is fate. Oh, they will be so happy when we see them." She turned back to Cam. "I nearly forgot to tell you the reason when I insisted on coming. I must speak to your cousin as soon as possible."

"Whatever for, *babushka*?"

"I have had more news." Her lower lip trembled. "About my dear Sasha."

"Who?" J.D. interjected.

Cam took a deep breath. For almost all his life, he'd heard about Sasha. "My grandmother's nephew," he said. "Grand Duke Aleksandr, the son of her eldest brother, the Crown Prince Ivan."

"Sasha is a nickname for Aleksandr," Natalia explained. "And my dear grandson was named after him. I was only ten years old when he was born, and I adored him." She laughed, though there was a distinct sadness in her eyes. "He was but a child when the rebels stormed the palace. We were to escape together. Me, him, and his mother. But we were separated. I can't remember why. I was running, and they were behind me and then ... they were gone. I tried to go back, but ..."

"Most of our research has led us to believe that mother and son had perished in the revolution—er, rebellion," he corrected when Natalia sent him a freezing glare. "Unfortunately, there is nothing left of the palace or the city."

"But he didn't die in the palace," Natalia insisted. "I know it. I can feel it. I don't know if he is alive now, but for many years, I could feel that he was somewhere in the world. And now I have proof that he lived on."

"Really?" J.D. asked. "What proof?"

Cam sighed inwardly. Growing up, he'd heard the all stories. And seen firsthand the effects of his grandmother's futile quest. For most of her life, she'd searched for the lost prince, and that attracted every kind of conman, charlatan, and impostor looking for a payout by taking advantage of a desperate woman's grief. "*Babushka*, we've been through this before—"

"Shush, Cam." J.D. held up a hand. "I wanna know more."

Natalia smiled at her gratefully. "I swear this time, my proof is irrefutable. A witness came to me, telling me that they had seen a dragon flying over a lake along the borders of Ukraine and Belarus, where Zaratena used to be."

"A dragon?"

"Yes. And so I said it must be my Sasha."

J.D. looked confused, so Cam explained. "My grandmother had a middle brother, Prince Peter. He was our official emissary to the Northern Isles, building our relations with them. In exchange, they sent one of their dragon guards to Zaratena to guard the Crown Prince and his family. It was a great honor. Prince Peter was in the Northern Isles when the rebellion happened, and the then-king, Aleksei's grandfather, gave him sanctuary. He married a local noble, and their daughter, Natasha, married the king's son, Harald, and became queen."

"What happened to the dragon guard in Zaratena?" J.D. asked, scooting to the edge of the couch.

"That's just it. He was lost too," Cam said. "Killed along with the prince and his mother."

"But don't you see? The dragon guard is still alive!" Natalia exclaimed. "There are so very few of them these days. Aleksei would be able to confirm if this dragon is the same dragon guard his grandfather sent long ago. If so, that means he's still protecting Sasha."

"If Sasha was still alive, he'd be old. Why wouldn't he come forward? Why—"

"Cam!" J.D. warned. "You're making your grandmother upset," she added in a low voice that only his shifter hearing could pick up.

He blew out a breath. "Look, I didn't mean to, but we must face the truth. It's been a long—"

"Hello, hello!" The door burst open. "Your Highness, I —" Arabella stopped short, a look of false surprise on her face. "Oh my. Apologies, I didn't realize you had company."

"What the hell is she still doing here?" J.D. snarled, shooting up to her feet.

"J.D., calm yourself," Cam urged, trying to tug her back down to the couch. Of course, his polar bear roared at him, vexed that their mate was upset by that horrible woman.

She slapped his hand away. "Calm down? You said she'd be sent away. That we'd never have to see her again!"

"Oh dear," Natalia said. "I'm sorry. This is my fault." The old woman shook her head. "Arabella has decided to stay."

"And why the hell—heck would you do that?" J.D. snarled.

"Because I have my own invitation to the Christmas ball." Arabella sauntered toward them, a smug smile on her face. "Well, my father, the Earl of Farthingdale does, but I RSVPed in his place, and since I was already in town, I decided to remain here. I'm staying in a suite one floor below."

J.D.'s face turned red. She looked like she was trying really hard not to explode.

Cam had no doubt that Arabella had screamed and cried to her father until the earl somehow found a way to get an invitation. The old git could never say no to his spoiled daughter.

"Arabella," he began as he stood up and put an arm around J.D. mustering as much coldness as he could. "This is a private moment." His polar bear, too, chuffed at her. It was angry because Arabella had upset their mate. "It's not proper for you to just enter Her Highness's suite when you wish." He made a mental note to tell Orson and speak with Natalia's head of security. "If you have business with my grandmother, you can make an appointment with her social secretary."

Arabella's nostrils flared and her lips pursed, but she shrank back. "As you wish, Your Grace." Her eyes looked J.D. up and down. "Nice outfit."

It was a miracle he didn't have to drag J.D. away as he could feel her cat ready to swipe its claws at Arabella.

When the door closed behind his former fiancé, Natalia

spoke up. "Perhaps we should continue our tea? J.D., *kotyonok*, please have a seat. Have you had real scones and clotted cream? I grew to love them in England, and I insisted Cook learn to make them from scratch."

J.D. took a deep breath and composed herself before sitting back down. "They look delicious."

Cam sat stiffly as they continued their tea, with small talk this time. There was no more mention of lost princes and dragons. Though it wasn't as intense as before, he could still feel his mate's seething anger. She was obviously angry at the whole situation, and he was kicking himself for thinking that Arabella would just go away without any fuss.

However, one thing that did reduce his worry was his grandmother's obvious acceptance of J.D. He smiled to himself at Natalia's name for J.D. *Kotyonok*. Kitten. Natalia had always had great instincts.

Finally, it was time to say goodbye, and he and J.D. stood up. "It was lovely to see you, *babushka*."

"Always, *lyuba*." She turned to J.D. "And you, *kotyonok*. I know you must be very busy, but perhaps you can visit me again soon before the ball?"

"Of course," she said. "And thank you ... for the food and tea and everything."

"Most welcome. And thank you for the gifts."

He embraced Natalia and kissed her on the cheek. "I'll come by tomorrow after work."

As soon as they left the suite, J.D.'s demeanor turned even more sullen. She was still mad at him, somehow, even though it wasn't his fault Arabella was here. He ran through a million things in his head of what he could do or say to her, but nothing seemed right. His ribs felt like they were being squeezed in, and J.D.'s silence only fueled his own anxiety. *What would happen now?* And how was he going to make things up to her?

They drove back to town, and since they hadn't talked about where they would go, he went in the direction of her house. In her current mood, he wasn't going to take any chances, and she probably needed some time alone. He would drop her off, and if she didn't want to speak to him, he would leave her for now.

His bear, however, disagreed. It urged him to make things right. It didn't care how, but it was unhappy at J.D.'s current mood.

We just need to leave her alone. Just give her some time. Maybe I can call Aleksei and ask him to un-invite Arabella. He and his second cousin were not close, but maybe—

"Sonafabitch!"

J.D. screeched when he slammed on the brake, her hand slamming on the dash as her seatbelt prevented her from careening forward. "What the hell, Cam?"

Anger seethed in him, threatening to boil over as he saw the familiar black pickup truck outside J.D.'s house. Not even bothering to turn off the engine, he flew out of his Range Rover.

Where the fuck is that bloody wanker? He wasn't in the truck, and so he proceeded toward the house. Sure enough, that bastard was there, standing on the porch. But what the hell was he doing?

As he got closer, he saw Roy at the door, a bucket at his

feet. He held a brush in his hand and was vigorously scrubbing at the wall. "What the— "

His vision turned red. His polar bear charged at his ribcage, wanting to get out. Though most of the vile words had been scrubbed off, he knew what it said. He crossed the distance between him and Jorrell with ground-eating steps.

"Did you do this?" he growled, grabbing the other man by the shirt and pulling him away.

"What the hell?" he exclaimed, whipping around, the brush flying from his hand. "Who—Oh, fuck you, man!"

The punch caught him off guard and hit him square on the jaw. "Why you—"

"Oh, not again! For crying out loud!" J.D. screamed, standing between them and herding him away.

"Look at what he did!" Cam cried. "Those words."

"I was trying to get them out, you buffoon!" Jorrell snarled back. Picking up the brush, he shoved it forward at Cam's face. "They were already here yesterday when she came home. Alone and barefoot," he added, just to rub more salt in the wound. "Just where the hell were you when this happened? I don't see you tryin' to help her."

"He's telling the truth, Cam," J.D. said. "Please. I don't want to do this right now."

A dark ugly feeling crept into his chest. "If I haven't made it clear yet, then let me state it in plain English. Stay. Away. From. My. Mate."

He spat and dropped the brush. "Yeah, whatever."

"Roy," J.D. began. "I'm sorry. I ... you didn't have to do this. I'm so sorry."

"It's all right, J.D." The look of tenderness he gave her made Cam want to rip his head off. "I was driving by, and I saw you hadn't cleaned it up. I had a bucket in my truck so I thought I'd save you the trouble."

Cam let out an inhuman roar, and he knew if that bastard didn't leave, his bear would rip out of him. "J.D.," he said through gritted teeth.

"You should go, Roy," she said. "Please."

The other man let out a snort, shot Cam a dirty look, then walked back toward his truck. As soon as he peeled off, he turned to J.D. "I suppose this is a taste of my own medicine."

"What?" The expression on her face was pure confusion.

"Him. And you and Arabella."

"Ara ... Oh my God! Are you jealous, Cam?"

"I'm not—" His bear roared so loud in his ears, his eardrums nearly burst. "Yes. Yes I am." He swallowed, feeling his previous words about how jealousy was unreasonable slide down his throat. "I'm jealous, all right? Happy now? Are you done being angry with me?"

"Cam." With a deep breath, she took his hands in hers. "Yes, I was jealous of Arabella. But not the way you think. And that's not why I'm upset." Light hazel eyes peered up at him as she lifted her head to his. "I did everything wrong today, didn't I?"

"J.D.—"

"No, no, you don't have to sugarcoat it," she said sheepishly. "I said all the wrong things, I did all the wrong things, hell, I even wore the wrong clothes."

"Natalia adored you. That's all that matters to me."

"Thank you. I adore her too. But ... that's not going to be enough, is it? To be ... by your side. When you take your place and do all the things you need to do. I'll have to attend parties with all kinds of important people. Probably host them, too. And meet more kings and queens than there are fingers on my hand. Arabella ... she ... she would be the kind of woman that could do all those things for you. I'm just a mechanic's daughter from Brooklyn."

"Don't." He wanted to tell her she didn't have to worry about anything. But J.D. was too smart for that, and he respected her too much to act condescendingly. "There's nothing you can do or say that would make me not choose to be with you."

"It's okay, really." She took a deep breath. "And I'm glad this happened. Because I'm not giving up, Cam."

"You're not?"

"No, goddammit." She placed her hands on her hips. "I'll do what it takes. I'll put on a fancy dress, learn how to say all the right things, have the manners and social grace. I'm going to be such a good mate for you that people will shoot rainbows out of their fucking asses if I ask them to."

There was a species of goats native to North America called myotonic goats. These goats had a peculiar genetic condition that made their muscles seize up when they were frightened, causing them to fall over, and thus many nicknamed them "fainting goats." J.D.'s declaration had scared and thrilled him at the same time that he couldn't move, as if his own muscles were suffering from *myotonia congenita*. So, he remained in place, staring at her for what seemed like eternity.

"Cam?"

As if it had been shot by lightning, his brain kicked into gear. "You're so fucking brilliant. And I love you."

This time, it was J.D. who seemed to have suffered from fainting goat syndrome, because her knees buckled from under her. His quick reflexes, thankfully, saved her from completely falling over. "Are you all right?"

"Did you just say ... that you ...you love me?"

"I do," he said. "More than you'll ever know."

She kissed him, mashing her lips into his hard. He returned the kiss with the same fervent ardor, sweeping his tongue into her mouth and tasting her sweetness. His admission only made the feelings he'd been keeping inside for so long burst out like a dam broke inside him, and he wanted her to know the depth and breadth of his love for her.

Neither of them pulled away for a while. Eventually, their biological need for oxygen overrode their passion and they broke off the kiss. "Let's go inside." She dragged him with her. "I need you. Now."

Chapter 13

J.D. knew she couldn't just turn into the kind of mate Cam needed on her own. No, she needed help. So, she called on the cavalry—that was, her friends—to help her look and act like a lady. They, of course, were more than happy to assist her, and next day, they all met at Dutchy's house.

"Don't you worry, J.D., we'll find you a dress," Dutchy assured her. "I have a few things in storage I can easily tailor, and if you don't like any of those, we can go to Aunt Angela's shop."

"And we'll find you the perfect lingerie to wear underneath," Sarah added. "Right, Darce?"

"Oh, definitely." Darcey clapped her hands together.

"Two questions." Gabriel had his hand up in the air. "First, what does it matter if she's wearing the right underwear? No one's going to see it."

"Because nothing makes a woman feel more powerful and confident than wearing sexy underwear," Sarah answered with a twinkle in her eye. "Trust me."

"All right. Well, second question, what the hell am I doing here?" Gabriel asked, scratching his head.

Beside him where they were cuddled on the couch, Temperance giggled. "Because J.D. trusts you, and she needs a male's perspective and opinion."

"Then why isn't Damon here?" Gabriel whined. "Or any of your mates?"

"Do we really want to get fashion or hair advice from my husband or those other guys?" Anna Victoria asked. "You're, like, the most qualified male among them, Gabriel."

"Well, when you put it that way—"

"Guys, come on," J.D. groaned as she dramatically plopped herself down on an armchair. "We have less than a week to get me ready for this shindig."

"I still can't believe Cam is related to royalty," Sarah said. J.D. had told them everything that had happened in the last two days, about Natalia, the business empire Cam was set to take over, and his relationship to King Aleksei.

"And he's a duke, too," Dutchy added. "Oh, I wish I could make a gown from scratch for you! But who knows, maybe you'll be the next one down the aisle."

"Whoa, whoa!" J.D. held up a hand. "Just because you got engaged doesn't mean I'm next."

"You better make an honest man outta him, McNamara," Gabriel joked. "Don't make me take out the shotgun."

"But you know that's the next step," Anna Victoria stated. "You're going to be presented as his mate. Why are you going to all this trouble if he's not going to put a ring on it? Has the bond formed yet?"

J.D. bit her lip. There had been no talk about marriage.

But he loves me. True, he hadn't said it again but then she hadn't said it back either.

It just didn't feel right at the moment. She wanted to be with him, that's why she was going to all this trouble—and to save his grandmother, of course—but the words just wouldn't make it out of her mouth. *Yet.* She would find the perfect moment to say it. But when?

"Come on now, guys," Darcey began. "We all know the mating bond is a personal matter."

J.D. smiled at the swan shifter gratefully. "Thanks, Darce. Everything's going so fast. One minute we were just taking things day by day and figuring out how we're going to make the long-distance thing work, and then next, I'm supposed to learn how to address royalty and curtsey and which direction I'm supposed to stir my tea with." With a loud groan, she sank deeper into couch. "God, what was I thinking? Cam is way out of my league. He plays three instruments, has two PhDs, speaks five languages—"

"So?" Sarah asked.

"I've been told I'm barely competent with this one."

"Stop, J.D.," Gabriel said. "You can't think like that. If anything, Cam doesn't deserve you." He held up a hand when she tried to protest. "J.D., I've known you longer than anyone here. Hell, probably longer than anyone else in the world aside from Damon. You've never had to change yourself for a man. Why are you starting now? Why can't you be good enough as you are?"

"I know that," she sighed. "But it's not just about me, remember? Am I supposed to just let his psycho family kill that sweet old lady?" Her heart clenched. She wasn't going to let anyone hurt Natalia, not if she could help it. "Anyway, can we just get on with it?" She looked at Anna Victoria. "You're still doing my makeup, right?"

"Of course," she answered.

"I'll help with the hair," Darcey offered.

"And I'll be here for moral support and pies," Temperance added.

Dutchy came over and put an arm around her. "It'll be fun. We'll all come here and get dressed and made-up together."

"It sounds like pure torture," she groaned. "But I'm glad you'll all be here with me. And that you're all coming to the ball, too. Maybe you all can take turns guarding me and making sure I don't make any more mistakes."

"C'mon now, J.D.," Dutchy said. "You know Sybil. She's nothing like those mean girls you knew back in high school."

"Yeah, it's everyone else I'm worried about. I don't wanna fall flat on my face and have everyone laugh at me."

The pressure surrounding the whole thing made her stomach turn sour. But she meant every word she said to Cam. She would do everything in her power, short of murder, to make sure she didn't embarrass him. God, she still cringed thinking about afternoon tea yesterday. She could feel his embarrassment, and she didn't want that for him.

Her cat sniffed, lifting its head in distaste.

Oh, shut up. She mentally rolled her eyes at her animal, but knew what it meant. It *had* hurt, that he felt embarrassed of her. But, that's why she had to turn herself into the perfect mate for him, so he never had to feel that way.

Besides, I'm a grown-ass woman. This was adulting, right? Not just paying her bills and shit. At some point, she would have to stop disgracing herself around other people. She was going to have to grow up and act like an adult.

The rest of the week passed by much quicker than J.D. anticipated. Work and getting ready for the ball took up most of her free time, but somehow, it all came together.

Dutchy pulled off a goddamn miracle and somehow found a dress J.D. actually liked. She hated everything else she had seen—they were all too girly, too itchy, too tight. It took her a few days of rooting around Dutchy's storage unit, but eventually, they found one that suited her.

The bright spots in her week were the times she spent with Cam and Natalia, having dinner together a few times in the latter's suite. In that short period, she'd come to adore the fierce, but loving old woman. She told them stories about growing up in the palace and her life before the revolution. But underneath the facade, there was sadness too. And though J.D. loathed Igor Dashokov's side of the family, it was obvious that marriage to the polar bear gangster was the only way she could have a normal life and a family of her own.

As her admiration and affection for Natalia grew, so did the pressure to make this work. Could she really do it? Be the perfect mate for Cam, be by his side as he took over his grandfather's legacy? What if she failed and fell—literally and figuratively—flat on her face?

She pushed away all the doubts and continued the mental countdown in her head to the Christmas Eve ball, willing it to come so she could get it over with.

Dammnit, she'd been so busy that she had actually forgotten it was nearly Christmas.

I don't even have a present for Cam, she thought.

They'd spent every night together, of course, usually at his place because it was closer to Natalia's hotel. He still hadn't said I love you to her again, but neither did she. It was just so hard to find a time, with everything going on around them. *After the ball*, she told herself. On Christmas morning. As soon as they woke up, snuggled together in bed, she'd tell him she loved him. It was the perfect plan.

The night of the ball finally arrived, and all the girls were in Dutchy's bedroom getting dressed, showered, and made-up. The men, on the other hand, were in the living room, watching sports and drinking beer.

"*Yeow*! That hurts! Jesus Johnnycake Christ, woman!" she cursed as Anna Victoria poked her eye with the fake lash she held up with a pair of tweezers. "Are you sure they haven't outlawed that in the Geneva Convention?"

With a defeated sigh, Sarah walked over to her, holding a glass jar filled with coins and bills. On the front, it was labeled Swear Jar. J.D. grumbled, pulled a crumpled dollar bill from her pocket, then shoved it inside. This was one of the methods her friends had employed to curb her bad cussing habit.

"At this rate, J.D.," Sarah began, shaking the nearly-full jar. "You're going to buy us all *two* rounds of drinks at The Den next girls' night."

"Now, now," Darcey soothed as she wrapped another of J.D.'s curls around a curling iron to help define the unruly locks. "It's just an eyelash. Hold your breath and sit still. I don't wanna burn you again."

"Yeah, Anders nearly tore the door down when he heard Darcey shout," Temperance reminded her.

"This isn't fair," J.D. pouted, crossing her arms over her chest. "Why do guys take five minutes to get ready, and we've been at this for hours, and we're still not done?"

"The trials of being a woman," Anna Victoria sighed. "Damon always complains about how long it takes me to get ready."

"All right, I'm done," Dutchy announced as she burst through the door. She'd had a few more adjustments to make to the dress after J.D. had tried it on and had retreated to her workshop. "Are you ready?"

"Let me finish up," Anna Victoria said. "We'll put your lipstick on when you're done."

Thankfully, Anna Victoria managed to apply the lashes without any more incidents or bloodshed. After getting into the silk and lace underwear and pushup bra Sarah had picked out, Dutchy helped her into her gown.

It wasn't really a gown in the traditional sense. Sure, it was all peachy-gold silk and satin, with a sweetheart neckline and a bow in the back. But the tiered skirt split in front, revealing that the outfit was a complete pantsuit underneath.

"Wow!" Temperance exclaimed. "J.D., you look gorgeous!" Everyone else oohed and aahed and gushed over the gown.

"See, I told you I'd get it done in time," Dutchy said, winking at her.

"Thanks, Dutch. I really couldn't see myself wearing anything else. It's so beautiful, but it's something I would definitely choose." She gave a turn, sending the shiny fabric swirling around her. "And it has pockets."

"Are you guys done yet?" Gabriel bellowed through the door. "The limos are here!"

"Hold your goddamn horses, Gabriel Russel!" J.D. yelled back. "We'll come out when we're done and ready."

"Oh boy," Anna Victoria slapped a hand over her head. "Where's that swear jar?"

"Don't worry, I'm tryin' to get it all out of my system now before we get to the castle," J.D. sighed. "Now let's go before Russel loses his shit."

Together, the girls left the bedroom and walked into the living room. All the men's gazes were fixed on the television as they watched a hockey game, but the moment their women entered, all five of them turned to them.

"Anna Victoria." Damon's emerald gaze fixed on his mate like there was no one else in the room. Anna Victoria wore a champagne gold gown with an embroidered torso and full skirt. "You look amazing," he rasped as he tucked a stray blonde lock away from her face.

"Sweetheart," Gabriel began as he approached Temperance. "I think you're going to make Queen Sybil herself jealous." The baker blushed and did a little twirl in her emerald green gown, sending the tulle skirt whirling around her like a cloud.

"Close that mouth or you'll catch flies, Rogers," Sarah quipped as Daniel gaped at her, slack-jawed. Her daring strapless red gown showed off the stained glass tattoo down her arm, and one toned, shapely leg peeked out from the slit down the side. "Didn't your dads tell you it's rude to stare?"

"Jesus, Darce, you look good enough to eat," Anders said, licking his lips and eyeing his mate in her light yellow, one-shoulder gown. "Let's skip the party."

Darcey giggled. "Are you sure? I might need you to help me find a bathroom or something."

The tiger shifter's expression turned funny, and he swallowed a gulp. "On second thought, you're right."

"Are you sure you'll be okay with the crowd, John?" Dutchy asked her mate. Her glossy red hair was pinned up in curls around her face, perfectly matching her vintage ice blue satin gown.

Krieger's normally serious expression was now one of awe as he gazed at her. "It'll all be worth it, seeing you like this tonight."

But perhaps the man who was surprised most of all was Cam. His blue-violet eyes pinned J.D. to the spot, his mouth parting, then closing, then parting again before he spoke. "J.D., you're ..."

If it weren't for her rib cage, her heart would surely have leapt out of her chest. "I clean up nice, huh?" And so did he, not that she expected anything less. Her mate looked like a dream in his black tux, his hair pulled back, and those gold-rimmed glasses perched on the bridge of his nose.

"More than nice, love." He leaned over and kissed her forehead. "You're absolutely stunning." His arm came around her, and his lips slid down lower to capture her mouth in a soft kiss.

"Don't mess up her hair!" Darcey cried.

"Or her lashes!" Anna Victoria added.

"S-sorry," Cam apologized as he took a step back. "Didn't mean to mess up your handiwork, ladies."

"Good thing she hasn't put on her lipstick," Temperance chuckled. "Or you'd be wearing it too, Cam."

Sarah winked at the polar bear shifter. "You're welcome. For later tonight."

"Welcome?" Cam asked, brows drawn together. "And what do you mean later?"

"Oh, you'll know," Sarah said mysteriously. "Actually, you're *all* welcome," she said to the rest of the men.

J.D. stifled a laugh. Earlier that evening, Sarah had given them all their Christmas gifts—matching sexy lingerie from her latest collection, not even out in the stores yet.

"All right, all right," Gabriel said as he clapped his hands and hustled everyone to the door. "Time to move, limos are waiting. We don't want to be late."

"Yes, carpool mom." Although she said it sarcastically, she flashed the lion shifter a grateful smile. "And, Gabriel?"

"What?"

"Thank you." She leaned over to kiss him on the cheek. "For getting all this together. And for everything else."

Gabriel's face softened. "Anything for you. But I hope you remember what I said before." His gaze dropped down to her bare arm, which Anna Victoria had covered up with makeup on her request.

It seemed like the right thing to do, since her tattoos didn't go with her dress, but from the disapproval on his face, she knew what he was thinking. Her stomach sank, but she pushed that feeling aside. *This is for Cam*, she told herself. *And Natalia.* "I know, I know."

"I mean it," he said firmly. "You're good enough, just as you are."

"I—sure." She nodded and swallowed the nervous lump in her throat as she tried to control the butterflies in her stomach. Her cat, too, was a bundle of nerves.

"Ready?" Cam said, placing a hand on her lower back.

With a deep breath, she smiled up at him. The love in his eyes sent a warmth through her, calming her and her animal. *Mine.* "Ready as I'll ever be. Let's go, champ."

Chapter 14

C am had seen many castles in Europe before, but to actually lay eyes on one in America was a sight to behold. "This is fascinating. It's as if someone took a castle from Austria or Germany and transported it whole to Colorado."

"You've never seen Blackstone Castle before?" J.D. asked as they alighted from their limo. "It's not part of your patrols?"

"Only the most senior rangers and Damon are allowed near here," he said. "For privacy reasons. Though I imagine that for the most part, everyone in Blackstone knows to avoid the dragon's lair."

"True."

They waited for the rest of their group to alight from their limos before heading into the castle. A formally-dressed butler greeted them and directed them toward the ballroom. Guests were already pouring in, but the presence of the dark-suited men with wired earpieces didn't escape Cam's notice. Human men.

"I knew security would be tight tonight," Cam said as they waited in the long line of people being checked before they could enter the ballroom. "But King Aleksei usually travels with his own Dragon Guards. Are these guys private security?"

"No, Secret Service," Damon said. "Vice President Scott Baker's in attendance tonight as well."

"Huh." *Strange.* The vice president had already visited Blackstone a few months ago. In fact, it made the headlines because there was an assassination attempt on his life, one that was foiled by Daniel Rogers.

"Did you know he was going to be here, Daniel?" Anders asked.

"Don't look at me." The bear shifter held his hands up. "I had no idea."

Thankfully the security procedures didn't take too long, and soon they were inside the ballroom. Crystal chandeliers lit up the entire room and garlands of evergreen with gold and red streamers stretched across the ceiling. Every corner was decorated with trees, boughs, holly, bells, ribbons and lights. One gigantic tree stood at the back of the room, and a bright star lit up the top. Waiters walked around carrying trays of canapés and champagne while a live orchestra played holiday music.

"You must be in heaven," Cam joked to J.D. "With all these decorations."

She whistled. "Yeah. It looks like Christmas threw up in here. In a classy way. I mean, you know, if Christmas ate champagne and truffles beforehand."

The corner of his mouth quirked up and he mentally

shook his head. J.D. really was one of a kind. And he loved every bit of her.

But did she feel the same way?

Don't be silly, he told himself. *Of course she does.* His bear agreed.

But she hadn't said the words. Not yet anyway, which is why the doubt was there.

His bear chuffed reassuringly. It was so close, he could almost feel and taste the bond, and surely, that wouldn't be the case if she didn't love him back. Perhaps she was just not the type to say the words. After all, she was trying so hard to make things work.

"I think I see your grandmother over there with Jason Lennox," she said.

"Excellent, let's go see her." They excused themselves from the rest of the group and headed to the alcove in the corner where J.D. had spotted Natalia chatting with the younger of the twin dragons.

"Cam," Jason greeted as they shook hands. They had met previously at the royal wedding, and even though he'd been living in Blackstone for nearly six months now, hadn't approached them until that night at the carnival. "Thank you so much for allowing me to escort Her Highness. Aside from my own mate, I don't think I have ever had a more beautiful and charming date."

"Oh, you flatterer." Natalia chuckled and playfully hit him on the shoulder with her fan. "If only I was a few decades younger."

Technically, Cam should have been his grandmother's escort, but he wanted to be with J.D., so he asked Jason and Matthew if they could take care of Natalia. It had actually worked out because Christina had just given birth a few days ago and was unable to attend the party tonight.

"Your Highness," J.D. greeted Natalia with a subdued nod. "Hey, Jason, how's Christina? And the babies?"

The dragon shifter's face lit up. "They're doing great," he grinned. "Pandora and Persephone are wearing us out, but I wouldn't have it any other way."

"Mr. Lennox has promised me I would be the first person outside the family to meet his twin girls," Natalia beamed. "Oh, I do miss holding babies."

When she shot a meaningful look at Cam, he only smiled back. For the first time in his life, he didn't mind his grandmother dropping hints. In fact, he himself had imagined it many times this past week. J.D.'s stomach growing large with their cub or kitten. Holding his child in his arms. Watching her nurture their son or daughter. His polar bear very much enjoyed all that.

"By the way, Cam," Jason took him aside and lowered his voice. "I need to talk to you about something later. I have news some—"

"Well, well, aren't we looking all cozy here?"

It was a good thing he had prepared mentally for Arabella's presence tonight. The pure joy he felt at having J.D. by his side would gird him for whatever poison she would fling. He wouldn't even give her the satisfaction of paying her any attention. However, it was hard to miss the way his grandmother's eyes grew large and her face turned ashen all of a sudden. "*Babushka?*"

"Aleksandr. Will you not greet me?"

Every muscle in his body stiffened, and his bear reared up at the sound of the heavily accented voice. Whirling around, disbelief shot through his brain for a moment, but he knew his eyes weren't deceiving him. "Hello, Uncle Stepan."

The older man's piercing light blue gaze bore right into him, his dominant polar bear like a lurking monster waiting within him. Stepan Dashokov was one his grandfather's five brothers, next oldest after Igor, and if rumors and whispers Cam had heard growing up were true, the one who objected the most to Igor's marriage to Natalia. Apparently, Stepan was bitter as he had always wanted to take over the family business from their father but had the bad luck of being born second after Igor.

"What a surprise to see you here, Stepan," Natalia said nervously. "And such a long way for you to travel."

"Yes, and since this is such a small, intimate gathering, I'm surprised you bothered to make the trip," Cam added. "Tell me, how did you manage an invitation?"

"MedvedDaz has many dealings all over Europe, including the Northern Isles. We are invited to a great many Christmas parties and affairs."

Though Stepan was technically vice president of the company, he was still in deep in the *other* side of the business. Transitioning to a legitimate operation was a process, after all, yet Cam couldn't help but wonder if his uncle dragged his feet in making that full transformation.

"And after all, we are family, yes?" Stepan continued. "How could I not come and see my dear sister-in-law and grand-nephew at the same time?"

"A missed opportunity, especially for someone so busy," Arabella added.

From the smug look on her face, Cam could guess exactly how Stepan found out about this party.

"Will you not introduce me to your ... friends?" Stepan raised a light brow and looked meaningfully at Jason and J.D.

"Of course." He swallowed, hoping to moisten his dry throat. "Uncle Stepan, this is Jason Lennox, one of our hosts tonight. Jason, this is my great-uncle, Stepan Dashokov."

"Mr. Dashokov. Welcome to Blackstone Castle." Jason's nod was polite, but his dragon displayed a flash of unmistakable dominance.

"Mr. Lennox. A pleasure to finally meet you." Stepan returned the nod and made no attempt at any posturing. "I have been trying to secure a meeting with Lennox Corporation for very long time now. Perhaps we can have a chat later?"

"I'm afraid you'll have to talk to my brother," he replied. "He's the CEO. I merely run the charity foundation. I'm not sure that'll be of any interest to you."

"Of course." His jaw ticked at the rebuff, but his face remained cool and unchanged. "And who is this lovely creature by your side, Aleksandr?"

"Uncle Stepan, my I present Ms. J.D. McNamara. My mate."

"Ms. McNamara. Lovely to meet you." Cam had no doubt that Stepan already knew who J.D. was, considering it was Arabella who had called him, but the totally unsurprised look on his face confirmed as much.

"Good evening, Mr. Dashokov." To her credit, J.D.'s expression was neutral, but he knew there was a storm brewing inside her, knowing that Stepan was part of the family who would harm Natalia.

"So, Aleksandr has found his mate," Stepan stated.

"He sure did," J.D. added. "Though *some* people might

wish otherwise. You know. Desperate people." Her gaze flickered at Arabella.

Don't let her get to you, he wished silently at J.D. *Please. Not tonight.* He knew his mate was not pleased that Arabella was here and obviously was responsible for the presence of his great-uncle. But all J.D. had to do tonight was smile and be polite, at least until this whole thing was over.

"Tell me, Ms. McNamara," Stepan began. "What is it you do?"

"I run a garage," she said.

"Garage?"

"She's a mechanic," Arabella interjected with a snort. "A tradesman."

"She owns the whole garage," Cam clarified. "She's a businesswoman."

J.D. stiffened at his side. "I fix cars, trucks, and motorcycles. It's a business, yes, and I get paid for what I do."

"Well, we all know what people who get paid for what they do are called," Arabella sniped.

J.D.'s face turned red. "Why you—"

The orchestra's horn section heralding the arrival of their guests of honor couldn't have come at a better time, and Cam sighed with relief as J.D.'s mouth snapped shut.

"If I may have everyone's attention," a voice boomed over the loud speakers. "Let us welcome, Their Majesties, King Aleksei and Queen Sybil of the Northern Isles." A round of applause erupted from the crowd.

"I'm glad they used the short version," Jason joked. "If they used all their titles, we might be here all night."

King Aleksei entered the ballroom, his queen consort on his arm. They made a striking couple with the king being so tall and elegant in his formal wear and Queen Sybil looking regally beautiful in a full-skirted silver ball gown. Flanking them on either side were two fierce-looking men whose eyes scanned the crowd, their presence effectively keeping people away.

"The famed Dragon Guards of the royal family," Stepan remarked. His normally stoic uncle sounded impressed.

"Why is there no receiving line? Does no one in this country observe proper protocol?" Arabella asked. "And why is no one else being presented? Princess Natalia should have been introduced before them, as the second-ranking royal. And before her, Cam, and any other members of the aristocracy."

Of course, what Arabella meant was that she wanted to be announced, a fact that didn't go over J.D.'s head. "The vice president's here, too, you know," J.D. said in an irritated voice. "And he's our second-ranked elected official here. In *America*."

Cam felt a headache coming on at the thought of being trapped between the two sniping women. But thankfully, Jason's diplomatic ways saved him.

"Sybil begged and pleaded that they make this informal," Jason explained. "Actually, she didn't want a ball at all, but seeing as they were visiting heads of a foreign state, there had to be some kind of social event. So, she and the State Department's protocol office made a compromise: no dinner or a receiving line and an announcement only."

The crowd parted and made way for them, and though this wasn't a formal state affair, they first made their way to Vice President Baker's party. They chitchatted for a while before turning toward Natalia.

"Princess Natalia," King Aleksei greeted. "How lovely to see you again. It's been such a long time."

Natalia curtseyed. "Your Majesties. Indeed, it has been a long time."

"You remember my great-aunt, don't you, Sybil?"

Queen Sybil smiled warmly. "Of course. Thank you for accepting our invitation. And welcome to Blackstone. How are you finding it so far?"

"Your birthplace and childhood home is a wonderful place, Your Majesty." Natalia answered.

"Your Majesty," Stepan said. "It is a pleasure to see you again. And your beautiful queen."

The dragon king's expression remained neutral, but the queen's posture turned rigid. "Stepan. Thank you for coming all the way just to meet us. Though it was unnecessary to travel so far as my trade ministers meet with you quite often."

"According to my social secretary, Mr. Dashokov was very insistent on giving us the honor of his presence," Queen Sybil added, her lips pursing. "How could we resist?"

Natalia smoothly slid into the conversation with a delicate clearing of her throat. "Your Majesty, you remember my grandson, His Grace, the Duke of Westmoreland? You met only once during your wedding."

"Of course," Sybil gave him a warm smile. "It's Cameron, right? Cam."

"Cousin Cam," Aleksei greeted. "It is nice to see you again."

"Your Majesty," he said, giving him a deferent nod.

Sybil looked to her brother. "Jason told us you were living here *and* working as a ranger! Why didn't you say anything?"

"I was quite surprised to hear that you were in

Blackstone, but then again, I should have known," King Aleksei said with a shake of his head. "Even though we were in Oxford around the same time, he much preferred mucking about the countryside doing his research rather than having pints with me at the pub."

Arabella cleared her throat, obviously not liking being ignored. She looked meaningfully at Cam.

Cam felt his stomach drop. Due to protocol, he would have to introduce Arabella before J.D., something his mate wouldn't understand. "Your Majesties," he began. "This is Lady Arabella Stepford-Price." Beside him, J.D. practically fumed. "She was gracious enough to accompany my grandmother on her long trip."

"Your Majesties," Arabella fawned, going down into a deep curtsey. "What an honor it is to meet you. It's a shame we had not met back when Cam and I were—"

The death glare he shot Arabella managed to shut her up. "And," he continued. "This is Ms.—"

"J.D.?" Queen Sybil's jaw practically dropped. "J.D. McNamara, is that really you?"

"Hey, Sybil, don't you look so *fiiiiine*," J.D. joked. "I mean, Your Majesty."

The queen broke away from Aleksei and pulled J.D. into a hug. "Oh my God! It really is you!" She laughed as she stepped back to look at J.D. "I didn't recognize you in that dress and the makeup. You look gorgeous! Not that you're not —I mean, no offense, I meant that in a good way."

"None taken, Sybil," she chuckled. "You look pretty damn—er, darn nice yourself. Your Majesty."

Arabella's nostrils flared. "I didn't realize you were acquainted."

"Her Majesty and I go way back." She put an arm around Sybil. "So, I hope you're not drinking and diving, now that you're a queen and all."

Queen Sybil smirked. "I've learned my lesson." The king shot her a questioning look and quickly, she explained to everybody how J.D. had rescued her when she was a pre-teen.

"Ms. McNamara," King Aleksei began. "If it were not for you, my mate would have perished, and we would not be here tonight."

"What? *Pshaw*." She waved a hand at him. "Anyone would have done it."

"Not just anyone," Sybil said. "No one at that party cared. Except you."

"Even though I did not know you or my queen back then, it seems I owe you a debt," King Aleksei insisted.

"Do you need a second Christmas tree?" The queen joked. "By the way, not that I'm complaining about seeing you, but what are you doing here?"

"Ah, my dear grandson has left out an important detail about Ms. McNamara," Natalia interjected. "She is his mate."

"Mate?" For the second time that evening, the queen looked flabbergasted. "You and Cousin Cam?"

"It's fate, isn't it, Your Majesty?" Natalia declared proudly. "It is meant to be. She saved the queen's life long ago, and now, she turns out to be the mate of your cousin."

Sybil squealed in a very un-queenly manner. "Ack! This is so cool."

Aleksei's mouth quirked up. "It is definitely fate. Congratulations, cousin. We must toast to you." Without even looking at them, one of the dragon guard flagged down a passing waiter, who distributed flutes of champagne. "To Cam and J.D.!"

"Cam and J.D.!"

Everyone took a sip of their champagne, though Arabella's lips barely touched the bubbly liquid as she sent poisonous looks at J.D. His mate, of course, shot her her best cat-that-ate-the-cream expression.

Sybil gathered J.D.'s hands in hers. "Join us for Christmas dinner tomorrow here, please?"

"You mean, I don't gotta eat Chinese takeout or pizza? Sure, we'll come."

"We can catch up as well, cousin." Aleksei put his hand on Sybil's waist. "Until then ..."

"Wait," Natalia said. "Please, Your Majesty. I must speak with you now."

Oh no, Cam thought, *not this again*. "*Babushka*, this is not the time." He reached out to put a hand on shoulder. "We can speak with Their Majesties tomorrow."

"*Bah*," Natalia brushed his hand away. "Time is running out. Who knows if the clues are still fresh at this point?"

"Cam, let your grandmother speak," J.D. said, and Natalia smiled at her gratefully.

"Fine." He let out a huff and shot Aleksei an apologetic look.

"What is it, Princess Natalia?" Aleksei asked.

"Remember what I told you? Of your Uncle Sasha? I have more news." Natalia told them about the dragon that had been spotted. "So, Your Majesty, don't you think it is worth investigating this claim?"

Aleksei thought for a moment. "Have you seen this dragon yourself?"

"I ... No. It was only relayed to me by a reliable source. But I know it." A hand went up to her heart. "I can feel it. The dragon and Sasha are connected."

"My dear aunt," Aleksei began, placing a hand on her shoulder. "I understand that after all these years, the loss of your—our dear Sasha has saddened you. But from what you have told me previously, you have been disappointed by these clues and stories before. Don't you think it's time that ... perhaps ... we should focus on what we have now." He motioned to J.D. and Cam. "And lay the past to rest."

Natalia's lower lip trembled. "But—"

"*Babushka*," Cam interrupted. "Perhaps—"

"No." All eyes turned to J.D. as she said that one word.

"Love," Cam began. "You—"

"*Nuh-uh*." She wagged a finger at him. "You don't get to decide how she feels or how to act. I believe you, Your Highness."

Natalia's eyes shimmered with tears. "Thank you, *kotyonok*."

Turning to Aleksei, she crossed her arms over her chest. "I'd like that favor now, Your Majesty."

Aleksei's blond brow rose up. "Favor?"

"Yeah, the debt you said you owe me."

"J.D.!" Cam warned. "Not now."

"Yes, now," she insisted. "Please. Your Majesty. Just ... just have someone check it out. I mean, surely you could send someone to investigate this lake." She gestured to the two burly guards behind him. "You got any more of those hunks? They look pretty capable."

The king continued to stare at her. "The Dragon Guards of the Northern Isles are the fiercest and most loyal warriors of my people. They are not errand boys."

Arabella snickered, which prompted J.D. to glare at her before turning to Aleksei. "Are you going back on your word? About that debt?"

"I—" Aleksei looked flummoxed.

The queen, on the other hand, suppressed a smile. "She's got your there, my king."

He let out a defeated sigh and closed his eyes. Immediately, one of his dragon guards stepped forward. The man was easily one of the tallest and widest men Cam had seen, dwarfing even the king. His hair was a shock of bright red, eyes a bright piercing green.

"This is Rorik," the king introduced. "Current Captain of the Dragon Guard. Rorik?"

"We shall endeavor to investigate the claims, Your Majesty," Rorik declared.

"Great!" J.D. clapped her hands together. "That's all we want. Thank you."

"You're welcome." Aleksei's expression turned amused as he and Cam locked gazes. "A mate should be someone to balance out your personality and complement yours. To make up for what you lack." He shook his head. "I wish you well, cousin."

"Don't worry, J.D., Princess Natalia," Sybil said. "I'll personally check in on the progress of the investigation for you."

"Thank you, Your Majesty." Natalia's voice choked up. "And thank you, *kotyonok*."

J.D. beamed at her. "You're welcome."

"Oh my," Arabella sneered. "Bribing a king. Surely there's a law against that somewhere."

J.D. turned bright red. "Who the hell asked you? Why don't you just shut your pie hole for once?"

"I'm positively shocked." Arabella's mouth shaped into an O, and a hand landed on her chest. "Tsk, tsk. Profanity is so unladylike."

Cam knew J.D. would not back down, so he placed a hand on her lower back, which was promptly shaken away. Anger radiated from her, and he could swear her cat swiped its claws at him.

"Is that so?" J.D.'s eyes narrowed into slits. "Oh, pardon me, your ladyship," she began in an exaggerated imitation of a posh British accent. "But would you be ever so kind, if it would please you, to *go fuck yourself.*"

"J.D.!" He grabbed at her hand, but she evaded him. "Your Majesties. My deepest apologies."

"Don't you dare apologize for me," J.D. warned, her face an alarming shade of purple.

Arabella, on the other hand, was obviously loving this turn of events. "Perhaps you and your little mate should excuse yourselves, Cam," she sneered.

He bit his lip. "Majesties. Your Highness. Uncle." He couldn't even look at his uncle's face. He could already guess the older man's disapproval at his mate's antics. Cam was supposed to elevate their status among the high society, and it was obvious J.D. would not be doing the Dashokov name any favors with her crass behavior.

J.D. turned on her heel and started walking away, not even waiting for him. He followed her through a set of glass doors that led to the outside. Hopefully, the cold air would temper her anger.

She stopped suddenly, her back remaining to him and so he, too, halted.

"Was that really necessary?" he asked. "Did you have to be so vulgar in front of the king and queen? And my family?"

She whirled around; face twisted in anger. "Your ex-fiancée started it!"

"But you didn't have to rise to her baiting! I thought you were smarter than this. Couldn't you have controlled yourself? I know you and the queen are friends, but you could have displayed some restraint in front of my uncle." Wasn't she the one who wanted to make this work? To ensure there was no cause for the Dashokovs to retaliate and put Natalia's life in peril? "Just this once, I wish you would think before you opened your mouth." The words flew out before he could stop them. From the look on her face, he knew he had unintentionally hurt her. His polar bear reared up in anger and began to tear his insides to shreds. "I didn't mean—"

"I thought maybe after tonight, I'd be done." Though her voice shook, she continued. "That I would magically change into this person that you needed me to be. But I realize now, I won't ever be done, will I? I'll never be good enough to stand beside you."

"No, J.D., please—"

"You know, everyone else laughing at me and calling me names, I can take. I've heard it my entire life and told each and every one of those people to fuck off. But you know what hurt the most, Cam? The fact that you didn't have my back in there. You, the one person I need most on my side, were ashamed of me. Well, let me tell you something, Cam! I'm not ashamed of me. I like me just the way I am, and I don't care what you, your snooty family, or anyone else thinks!"

Her words had hit their mark, like darts pinning him into place. He couldn't move, not even to stop her as she brushed past him to go back into the ballroom.

While he may have justified his actions because his uncle was there, she was hurt nonetheless. And it was true, he did feel embarrassed at her antics.

But he was wrong to criticize her or make her feel like she had to change to be with him, as if who she was wasn't good enough for him.

"Bloody hell!" He pressed a palm to his head as dread crept into his chest. He had hurt her so deeply. The woman he loved. *I'm a fucking bastard.*

His bear agreed wholeheartedly, then urged him to go back inside. *I know we have to get her back.* He had to apologize to her right away. Tell her he was wrong, grovel on his knees if he had to.

However, mere words would mean nothing to her. He had to think of something else. Something big. A gesture so grand, she wouldn't be able to ignore it. But what?

As he re-entered the ballroom and the music of the orchestra blasted into his eardrums, an idea struck. Of a grand gesture he could do to win her back.

His heart drummed as anxiety filled him at the thought of what he was about to do. There were so many people here. They would be watching. And she could still reject him, and the bond would never form. But, at this point, he had nothing to lose.

Chapter 15

J.D.'s body vibrated from rage and humiliation, but she swore to herself she wouldn't cry. Her damn chest ached like someone had buried an axe in there, but she willed herself to get ahold of the tears burning in her throat. Feeding the anger growing inside her was the only way to stop the deluge threatening to burst out.

She rushed out of the ballroom and down the hallway to the women's powder room. Thankfully, it was empty at the moment, so she turned the lock behind her, then leaned back and let out a calming breath.

I thought I could do it.

She'd tried so hard. But none of it was good enough for Cam. She thought getting dressed up and attending this stupid ball would make her good enough. But his actions tonight had told her otherwise. She would never be the mate he needed her to be.

Sure, she could have stayed meek and quiet, but that wasn't her. She could probably look over the fact that he didn't introduce her first or that he didn't defend her when

Arabella started acting like a bitch. But the worst part was feeling his embarrassment at her actions and apologizing for her when she was only defending herself.

Her cat hissed and seethed. It wanted to get out, pounce on that bitch and claw her eyes out. And J.D. was sorely tempted to let it.

"J.D.?"

The knock at the door startled her and jolted her out of her thoughts.

"J.D.? Are you in there? I saw you walking this way."

Natalia. She wasn't ready to face her. Or anyone. So she remained quiet.

"I know you are in there, *kotyonok.*"

Damn. "I'm uh ... I'm not entertaining right now, Your Highness. Please leave me alone."

"J.D., I order you to open this door at once!"

The tone in Natalia's voice made her stand up straight and hair rise on her arms. "All right, all right." With a deep sigh, she turned around and opened the door. "What can I do for you, ma'am?"

Natalia sighed. "I saw you running out of the ballroom and my grandson nowhere in sight. I knew the situation was not good. What happened?"

She considered lying to the old woman, but she doubted she would believe it. "It just ... it's not working out, Natalia. Cam and me."

"Not working out? But you are mates. Fated to be together. I do not believe it!"

"Well, I don't know what to tell you. We just had a big fight, and I don't think there's any way we're going to make up." Her shoulders slumped. "It was never going to work out.

We're just too different. We come from different worlds. And I should have known we would never get along, the moment he showed himself to be a real Scrooge."

"Scrooge?"

"You know. A Christmas Carol. The guy who hates Christmas."

Recognition flashed in the old woman's face. "Ah. Charles Dickens. But what—" She sucked in a quick breath. "Ah. I see now. Come, *kotyonok*."

J.D. found herself being dragged toward the small couch in the corner. "Sit," Natalia ordered, "and let me tell you something."

"If this is about how Cam didn't mean anything he said—"

"Shush, I am speaking." Natalia's eyes narrowed at her, and J.D. closed her mouth. "Aleksandr—Cam," she began, "was not your typical child growing up. He told you about his parents?"

"Yes."

"Edward, Cam's father, resented his father for arranging the marriage with my Anastasia. However, they had no choice because the creditors were at the door, ready to strip them of what they had left. My husband's money was the only thing that saved their estate. But the truth was, Edward himself was no better than his father. A drunkard who drank even more as his resentment grew. And a wastrel who blew through my daughter's dowry in a year. Thank goodness my husband's pockets were deep, and he made sure that the purse strings were kept out of Edward's reach when he set up Anastasia's trust fund. Igor had hoped he would change when Cam was born. But ... he only got worse. See, Edward also hated the fact that Anastasia and Cam were shifters."

Her cat let out an angry hiss. "What? Cam's dad hated shifters?"

"Yes. This was a fact he didn't realize until after the betrothal contract was signed and he had no choice. He was ... disgusted by the idea that he was marrying a shifter."

"Sonofabitch! Er, sorry."

Natalia patted her hand. "Do not worry. I said worse when Anastasia relayed this to me. When Cam was born, Edward didn't hide his bitterness and animosity. He was cruel to Cam. He never hurt him, but never showed him affection either. When he was learning to shift, Edward would berate him whenever he had any accidents, like if he changed into his bear inside the house or scratched up his furniture. He even started forcing Cam to wear those glasses to hide that glow in his eyes when his bear came to the surface. And then Anastasia died in that car crash." Tears streaked down Natalia's cheeks as she sobbed, and J.D. rushed to the sink to grab some tissues. "Thank you. Apologies. You never really get over the death of a child."

"It's all right," she soothed. "Take your time."

Natalia blew her nose into the tissue and wiped her tears. "No, I must continue. So you can understand. When Anastasia died, Edward didn't even want Cam to live with him in his manor, so he was sent away to boarding school a few weeks after her funeral. He was nine years old."

Her chest tightened as she imagined Cam losing him mother and being kicked out of the only home he knew.

"And after that first year, when all of his peers left for Christmas break, he was left behind."

"What?"

"Edward refused to pick him up for the holidays. He had to spend it at St. Andrew's. I didn't even know about this, otherwise I would have insisted he come live with me instead. But I had no rights. Edward was still his father. He wouldn't even sign the papers to let me take him for the holidays or so I could visit. He would probably have left Cam there during the summer, too, if the school was open. That was the only time I got to see him."

Oh, Cam. Tears sprang to her eyes. No wonder he hated Christmas. While he got to see everyone go home and be with their families, he was left alone in that boarding school. Who could blame him? She'd seen the anxiety in his eyes. How hard it was for him to open up.

"Worse still, Edward remarried and had a daughter. But because Cam had been born first, the title would eventually pass over to him, which made him resent Cam even more. He spoiled his new daughter, spent every holiday with her until he died." Natalia didn't seem too broken up about that. "I thought Cam would get over it, I did my best to make sure he knew he was loved."

"And you did," she said. "And he loves you so much."

"He's always been indifferent about the holidays. When he left St. Andrews, he would always spend them alone. And then ... then Arabella happened. He was happy with her. She's a lovely girl. But they broke up on Christmas five years ago, and I think that made him even hate the holidays more."

Rage boiled inside her and she wanted to scream the truth at Natalia. That they didn't just break up, but Arabella had cheated on him. *Stop*, she told herself. That wasn't her story to tell.

"So, you see? My grandson has never had a reason to celebrate the holidays. He's always been withdrawn and cold, focused—no, obsessed with his work. He prefers the company of his animals and plants because he's afraid of interacting with people and being hurt and disappointed by them." The old woman's weathered hands covered hers. "But these past few days, I've seen the change in him. Something in his thirty-six years that I haven't seen before. True happiness and love, at least when he looks at you."

J.D. couldn't breathe. She was so afraid that if she made even the smallest motion, she would burst into tears. She wanted to believe Natalia's assessment, she really did. But his actions were still too fresh, and she didn't know if she could trust him.

"Please, J.D.," Natalia begged. "Would you please speak with him? Just have a conversation."

"I ... I'm scared," she admitted.

"He's hurt you. And I understand your hesitation. But surely, you could find it in your heart to hear him out and let him apologize."

"You don't even know if he's sorry for what he did and said."

"I know my grandson and that he would do anything for you. Please."

Conflicting emotions swirled within her. Her brain told her to run away now, before she got even more hurt. But her stupid heart and her inner animal wanted to hear him out. "I ... I suppose we could talk."

"Thank you." Natalia leaned over and kissed her on the cheek, then stood, dragging her up. "Come. We should go."

"I—"

The old woman pulled her along before she could protest further. When they returned to the ballroom, Natalia stopped. "Stay here. I will look for Aleksandr and send him to you, yes?"

"All right."

As the old woman disappeared into the crowd. J.D. considered running away. Just going home, changing into her pajamas, and waiting for this damned day to be over.

"Well, well, look what the cat dragged back in," Arabella scoffed as she sauntered over. "When I saw you running away, I truly thought we had seen the last of you. But I guess pests are always hard to get rid of."

Fucking bitch. But she was not going to let this heifer rile her up again. "I bet that's what all your ex-fiancés say when you come crawling back."

Arabella's pretty face twisted into an expression of hate. "Go ahead and keep insulting me. But the truth is you'll never belong here, in our world. You'll always be a poor grease monkey. What's that American saying? About putting lipstick on a pig?"

Her cat hissed and let out its claws, but she reined in it. "Better a poor grease monkey than a lying, cheating bitch like you."

"Oh, so he told you the real reason we broke up?" Arabella snorted. "Tiago and I had a little fling while I was wearing Cam's ring, so what? It's ancient history and Cam will forgive me in time. Now that he realizes that you can never be what he needs to live up to his legacy. I, on the other hand, will be the perfect wife for him."

"Excuse me," Natalia began, clearing her throat.

Arabella's complexion turned ashen. "Your Highness!"

She whirled around to face Natalia. "Th-there you are. I was looking for you everywhere."

"Apparently, you look for a great many things everywhere. Even in places you should not be looking." From Natalia's cold, freezing stare, it was obvious she had overheard everything. "Lady Arabella, I think perhaps it's time you leave."

"But, I—"

"That was not a suggestion."

Her lips pursed and eyes narrowed. "You wrinkled old hag, you deserve what's coming to you," she spat, then turned to J.D. "The Dashokovs will never accept you. But then again, you're all animals, the lot of you."

"Leave now before I fucking kill you, bitch!" J.D. hissed. To make her point, she opened her mouth and let out an inhuman growl.

Arabella jumped back. "Fine. I'm leaving. You deserve each other." Lifting her head, she turned and marched out of the room.

Natalia shook her head. "Why didn't Cam tell me?"

"He didn't see the point," J.D. said. "He knew it would hurt you."

"*Bah*. I hate cheaters. Igor and I may not have been mates or madly in love in the beginning, but he vowed never to betray me with another woman. Polar bears are fiercely loyal to their other halves." There was a softness in her face that made her seem decades younger. "Anyway, good riddance to that vile woman. We will never have to think about her again."

"I hope so." If she saw Arabella again, it would be too soon.

Natalia's face brightened. "I nearly forgot! I came to tell you that I found my grandson. But he's indisposed for the moment, but asks that I ensure you do not leave."

"I'm not sure ... Arabella, what she said about the Dashokovs ... it's true, right? Cam should be with someone refined and graceful like her."

"What nonsense," Natalia declared. "Fate has paired him with the mate he needs."

"Please, I should—"

"Shush."

"But I—"

"I said, shush!" Natalia gripped her hand. "Stay quiet and listen."

"Listen?" She cocked her head. "Listen to what?"

Natalia lifted a finger in the air. "To that."

The orchestra had stopped playing some time ago and after a few more seconds of silence, music began to fill the air. Piano music.

Every hair on her arm and neck stood on end as J.D. recognized the opening notes of Billy Joel's "Just The Way You Are."

Natalia smiled at her and pulled her along, toward the raised dais next to the orchestra. Sure enough, Cam sat behind the piano, tinkling out the intro and the first few bars.

And when their eyes met, he began to sing.

His eyes never left hers as he worked through the song. Those lyrics that she knew so well began to embed itself into her heart as Cam's beautiful voice wove its magic around her, surrounding her and filling all the empty places in her heart and soul she never even knew had been there. His voice called to her, reached out to her, begged for her forgiveness with each note and word.

She didn't know what it was, but it was as if she could feel his sincerity, his love, and his very soul, knitting into hers. Her heart sang along, repeating the words back to him. So simple, yet so true.

When he finished the song, the room was completely silent. Slowly he stood up. "I'm sorry, J.D.," he began. "Please forgive me. You don't have to change anything about you. In fact, I'd prefer it if you don't because I love you just—"

She didn't let him finish as she flew to him, wrapping her arms around him, then kissed him with all her might and love. "I love you too, Cam," she said, breathless. "You felt it right? The bond? It really happened."

He blinked. "You're right. Fascinating."

His expression was similar to that of a little boy who just discovered something new. And she loved it. "Weirdo." But she kissed him again. Around them, everyone cheered.

Cam tried to pull away, but she wouldn't let him. She only deepened the kiss, clinging to him as she ravaged his mouth. Finally, when someone behind them coughed, she released him. "Your glasses are all fogged up again."

Letting go of her, he took them off. But instead of cleaning the lenses, Cam chucked them over his shoulder. "Don't need those anymore. Maestro," he said to the orchestra leader. "If you please."

The conductor nodded, raised his baton, and turned to the musicians. "One, two, three and—"

J.D. burst out laughing as they began to play another familiar, but more upbeat Billy Joel tune. "So," she began, wrapping her arms around his neck. "Does that make you my Uptown Boy?"

"I'll be your anything," he said. "As long as you're mine. Now, let's dance."

And Cam showed her that he wasn't just a good pianist and an excellent singer, but was also talented on the dance floor.

Chapter 16

As they danced the night away under the glittering chandeliers, evergreen, and boughs of holly, Cam still couldn't believe this was all real. If he were the type to believe such things, he would have called it a Christmas miracle. However, even his scientific mind was willing to concede that this was, indeed, fate at work.

Whatever it was, he sent silent prayers to whatever force in the universe had given him J.D. Through the mate bond they shared, he could feel the love and joy flowing between them, and he had never been happier in his life.

Of course, he knew this was only the beginning. There was much work to be done in the next few months as he made his transition. Though a cloud of gloom hung over him at the prospect of leaving a career he truly cared about, having J.D. at his side would ease that sadness.

"Why so glum?" she asked as they stopped to drink some more champagne a passing waiter handed them. They had danced with just about everyone that evening, pulling their friends onto the dance floor. She even managed to get his grandmother into her very first conga line.

"Nothing ... just tired," he assured her. "You've kept me on my feet all night."

"Hmm ... well how about I just get you on your back for the rest of it?" She wiggled her eyebrows at him suggestively.

He knocked back the champagne. "Where's that limo?"

"C'mon," she said with a laugh as she tugged him toward the door. They laughed and kissed as they made their way outside of the castle.

The driveway was empty, as many of the guests had already left and it was nearly midnight. "Gabriel said he'd send the limo back for us. I wonder—" Cam halted as he felt a presence in the shadows. He stopped as his polar bear reared up, and instinctively, he put his body in front of J.D.'s.

"Cam?" she asked. "What's wrong?"

Someone stepped forward from the shadows a few feet away from them. "Hello, J.D. Did you have a nice time at your fancy party?"

"Roy?" J.D. exclaimed.

Cam's body went on full alert. This wanker again. He would deal with Jorrell right this instant. "What the fuck are you doing here? I told you to stay away from my mate."

His expression turned to full on hate as he zeroed in on Cam. "You're not her mate," he spat. "*I* am."

His bear roared in anger. "You delusional twat. I'm going to kill—"

"You're mistaken, Roy," J.D. interrupted. "I'm not your mate. Cam is my mate."

"No!" he roared. "That's not true. I can feel it. You know I'm your mate."

Cam's anger was about to boil over, but J.D. put a hand on his arm.

"I'm sorry, but it's not. We would have known the first time we met."

"But we were kids," Jorrell reasoned. "We weren't mature enough."

"Then our animals would have recognized each other a few weeks ago when you walked into my shop," she pointed out.

"Search your heart, J.D." Roy pleaded. "I didn't realize it back in high school, but now I know it."

"But my cat doesn't recognize you as its mate. Does yours recognize me?"

"I ..." His eyes turned crazy. "My raven doesn't know shit, okay? You were always so nice to me. I knew there was a reason. We were meant to be—"

"All right, this stops right here, right now." Cam's voice shook with anger. "Leave now, and never come near her or me again."

"Or what, huh, pretty boy?" he threatened. "What are you going to do? You know what, you're right. This stops here. I challenge you for J.D."

"What the fuck is this shit?" J.D. shouted. "Are you for freaking real, Roy? Are you drunk or high? Go home and sleep it off."

"What the fuck is going on here?"

They all turned around at the sound of the dominant voice. Jason Lennox stood at the doorway arms crossed over his chest. "Who the hell—you." His eyes glowed as they zeroed in on Jorrell. "We've been looking for you, Roy."

"Looking for him?" Cam asked.

Jason took a step forward, eyes fixed on the other man "Well, remember that kidnapping attempt on J.D.? When Roy's description of the perpetrators didn't pan out, we continued our search. Went to some of the businesses across the street from the park and found some CCTV footage of two men on motorcycles driving away around the time of the kidnapping. Tracked them down, and it turns out they were hired specifically to target J.D."

"Hired?" J.D. asked. "By who?"

"Who else?" Jason nodded at Jorrell. "Your knight in shining armor. Tell me, Roy, was the plan to rescue her and turn yourself into a hero or something worse?"

Jorrell paled. "I-it's not what you think, J.D."

"You bastard!" Cam roared. "You did all those other things, too, right? Sent her the gifts? Vandalized her front door so you could come in and clean it up to make yourself look good?"

"You asshole!" J.D. snarled at Roy. "If I was your mate, you wouldn't do those things."

Roy's expression turned hateful. "I'm not backing down. The challenge stands," he said to Cam.

"What? Listen here, fuck face," J.D. began. "That's not how it works."

"Challenge accepted," Cam said as he slipped off his jacket.

"Challenge—what the hell, Cam!" J.D. cried. "You can't duel for me!"

"This is the only way he'll accept defeat." He handed his jacket to Jason, who took it, then began to roll up his sleeves.

"That's hardly fair," she pointed out. "You're a polar bear, and he's a raven."

"I can take him," Jorrell spat.

"And I don't need to shift," Cam added. "I can beat this wanker with one hand tied behind me."

"Oh God, is this really happening?" J.D. buried her face in her hands. "Fine, go ahead. Don't listen to me."

Cam kept his focus on Jorrell as they stepped into the driveway, circling each other. Oh, he was going to enjoy beating this man to a bloody pulp.

Jorrell whipped off his shirt, and he flexed his muscles. Though he was shorter than Cam, he was in excellent shape. "After I sold my app in high school and became a multimillionaire, I left Blackstone to travel the world," he boasted. "I started training with the best fighters all over the world. I learned Muay Thai in Thailand. Karate in Japan. Jiu-jitsu in Brazil. Krav Maga in Israel. So," he put his fists up. "Bring it on, pretty boy."

What Jorrell didn't know was part of Cam's summer training in Russia while he was growing up was wrestling and fighting with his polar bear cousins, many of them bigger and meaner than this wannabe fighter. "Oh, I'll 'bring it'." He lunged forward.

Jorrell quickly moved to dodge his hold. Cam whirled around to face him, ready for a counterattack. Though the raven shifter had caught him with a kick to the side, he didn't flinch. He'd been so used to the pain his cousins inflicted on him, he knew when to tense his muscles to absorb the blow.

That seemed to catch his opponent off guard as he probably expected Cam to double over. Using this to his advantage, he lunged again, taking Jorrell down to floor, flipping him over, and putting him in a sleeper hold.

"Yield!" Cam ordered.

Jorrell screamed, spittle flew from his mouth, but he didn't tap out. "Fuck you!"

"I said," he tightened his hold. "Yield!" His polar bear roared, sending a rattling growl ripping from his throat.

His opponent yelped, then tapped a hand on the ground. "I ... yield!"

Cam squeezed his neck until he passed out. "Bastard." He got to his feet, brushing the dust and dirt off his shirt.

"Cam, you idiot!" J.D. exclaimed, then wrapped her arms around him.

"You didn't think he could defeat me, did you?"

She snorted. "Of course not, I had full confidence in you. But I can't believe that you would ... that you could—"

"Fight for you?" he finished. "No one tries to steal what's mine and gets away with it."

Her pupils blew up as she melted against him. "Wow, Spenser ... that was kind of hot. I think I need to be alone with you. Like, right now."

"Well, I can arrange—"

"Aleksandr."

He winced inwardly. "Uncle Stepan," he greeted the older polar bear shifter. He stood next to Jason by the doorway, along with his grandmother. How long had the old man been there?

"I already called my driver and offered Princess Natalia a ride back since we were both staying at the same hotel." He nodded at the limo that pulled up. "I did not expect to see a show."

Cam sent an apologetic look to Natalia. "I'm sorry you had to see that, *babushka*."

"*Bah*," she exclaimed. "I have seen much violence in my lifetime."

"I must admit," Stepan said, light eyes piercing into him. "I did not think you had it in you."

"I didn't kill him, just incapacitated him."

"You fight for what's yours. Defend what belongs to you. That is impressive."

Had he been transported to another dimension? Did Stepan Dashokov actually compliment him?

"What did you think he was going to do?" J.D. asked. "Back down? Cam is smart, brave, and strong."

Stepan's laser-like gaze zeroed in on J.D. "'Though she be but little, she is fierce.'"

"Shakespeare," Cam said. "*Midsummer Night's Dream*."

"You seem surprised that I know that quote. What, you think you're the only one who reads? So, little cat," he said to J.D. "I have this feeling you've been sharpening your claws, waiting to swipe at me. What have I done to you to deserve such hatred?"

"It's not what you've done to me," she began, "but what you're forcing Cam to do."

"J.D," Cam began. "You don't have to do this."

"But I do," she said. "This blood oath business, threatening your grandmother, forcing you to give up a career you love, possibly sentencing me to a life of dinner parties and balls. He needs to answer for it."

"Blood oath?" Stepan sneered. "Why would I care for that?"

"Isn't that why you're here?" J.D. asked. "Why Arabella told you about this ball? So you could come and ensure Cam would be fulfilling the blood oath of your brother? And that his mate would be worthy enough to bring honor to your name or whatever shit deal he made with you and your family?"

Stepan's cool expression didn't falter. "I must admit, I was intrigued when that silly Englishwoman contacted me. I had to see for myself what kind of man Aleksandr turned out to be and what mate fate had chosen for him."

"I'm sure you didn't expect me," J.D. said.

"I did not." But there was a hint of amusement in his tone.

"I'm not the perfect, blue-blooded mate you were hoping for the man who's about to take over the family company, am I? Sorry to disappoint you."

Stepan huffed. "My brother was the one obsessed about pedigree. He seemed to be intent on erasing our past. Before our coffers grew and our power expanded. To forget about those cold, winter nights we spent huddled on the cold floor of whatever rat hole shelter our father managed to find us for the night. The blue bloods turned us away when he begged for a morsel even while they had so much. But I recall it was working men, the tradesmen—the grocers, the electricians, the truck drivers, and yes, the mechanics, who, despite what little they had, would always have a piece of bread to share with us or space by their hearth to keep us warm. It was *those* people I did not forget."

"Stepan," Natalia began. "Igor, may God rest his soul, helped grow this empire we all benefit from. But ... we must accept that he is gone, and perhaps ... we do not have to adhere to the wishes of an old man."

Stepan immediately understood Natalia's words. "I see."

Hope soared in Cam's chest, giving him the courage to speak up. "I know I was groomed to take over the company. And that it was grandfather's wish and fulfillment of the oath he made to you and your brothers."

"A blood oath cannot be broken," Stepan stated. "Igor was to produce an heir to take over the business."

"Well, it seems to me that he already fulfilled his oath," J.D. continued. "He did sire an heir—Cam's mother. No one said it had to be a male heir. Unfortunately, she died before she could take over, right? There was no mention of what were to happen if the heir died, and no promise of her grandchildren fulfilling the oath. Just the heir."

Stepan thought for moment. "Yes, it seems you are right."

J.D., you are a bloody genius! He wanted to kiss her right now, but held back.

"Aleksandr," his uncle began. "If you have no objections—"

"None," he interrupted. "None at all. You can take the lot of it—I mean, I relinquish any control or claim over the company holdings."

"It's not as easy as that," Stepan said. "There is paperwork to be done. Announcements to the rest of the family."

"I'll do whatever it takes."

"You shall retain your shares, of course."

They could bloody take them all and hand over one ruble to him and he'd be more than happy. But there was one thing left. "And of course, my grandmother's safety is ensured?"

"Of course," Stepan nodded. "She is released from the blood oath."

"Yes!" J.D. cried and hugged Natalia. "Oh my God! I'm so relieved!"

Cam, too, felt like a giant weight had been lifted off his shoulders, one he'd been carrying around since birth. "Thank you, Uncle." He was sure, however, that it wasn't a hardship for Stepan. He'd probably been waiting for decades for a chance to take over. After all, he had young, strong sons of his own, and would want to see them eventually rise up in the world.

"Well, this has been an exciting evening," Stepan said. "I must go and make a few phone calls."

"I shall stay for a while longer with Aleksandr and J.D.," Natalia said.

"Of course. And if I do not see you before I leave, I bid you goodbye." He bowed to Natalia, nodded to Cam and Jason Lennox, and to his surprise, winked at J.D., before he walked toward the waiting limousine.

Cam turned to Jason. "I'm guessing you know what to do with this trash?" He said, motioning to the still-unconscious form of Roy Jorrell.

The dragon shifter's eyes glowed. "You bet." Walking over to the prone form, he picked up Jorrell with one hand. "I'll lock him up in one of the closets until the police get here."

Cam let out a distasteful snort when they disappeared into the castle. "Good riddance." His polar bear was satisfied for now, but it was still agitated because that man who hurt their mate and attempted to steal her was still breathing.

"Aleksandr," Natalia embraced him. "For years, I've seen you grow sad and bitter, but you accepted your fate because of the blood oath."

His throat closed up. There was always that tension between them, that unspoken thought that he was doing what he was supposed to because he didn't want her to die. "I would have gone through with it. Whatever it took. A thousand times if I had to, to keep you safe."

"I know, *lyuba*," she said, tears in her eyes. "But now, you can finally live your own life. I'm so happy for you. And for your mate."

"Thank you." He pulled J.D. close to him. "I love you, J.D.," he whispered. "Thank you. For everything."

"And I would have gone through with it, too, you know," she said. "I'd follow you to the ends of the earth. Put on the most uncomfortable gowns and the highest heels for you. Talk to the most important and boring people on earth and muzzled my potty mouth."

"Now I know you really must love me," he quipped.

"I do, you weirdo." She sighed. "I guess we'll have to find a way to make ends meet on your ranger salary, huh?"

"I suppose we'll have to tighten our belts." Of course, between his trust fund and the value of his shares in MedvedDaz, neither of them had to work another day in their lives.

"You can live with us, Your Highness," J.D. put an arm around Natalia. "I have a spare room for you. We'll decorate it with some nice curtains."

Natalia laughed. "I would be happy to make use of your room for a visit, but I think it will be more useful as a nursery, eh? And really, you must call me *babushka* from now on."

"*Babushka*? Hmmm. Too long." She tapped a finger on her chin. "We'll figure out another nickname for you. I—oh crap."

"J.D.? What's wrong now?" Cam asked, his polar bear going on full alert.

Her hands slapped over her forehead. "I almost forgot! It's Christmas!"

"Christ—oh." He looked at his watch. It was already past midnight. "You're right. Merry Christmas, love." He pulled her close.

"Merry Christmas. But I forgot to get you a present," she whined. "And this is our first Christmas together."

The love in his heart filled his chest with much lightness and warmth, and using the bond, he pushed that feeling to her. Her eyes lit up with recognition.

"Love," he began, kissing her square on the mouth. "You've already given me the best Christmas present of all."

"And this is the bestest, most perfect Christmas ever," she said, then pouted. "Well, almost a perfect Christmas."

"Almost?" he said in a mock offended tone. "I serenaded you in a crowded ballroom to declare my love *and* dueled for your honor! How much more perfect of a Christmas could this be?"

"Weeeellllll, we just need some—" She gasped, her eyes lighting up as they grew wide.

"Love? What's wrong?"

"Look." She nodded at the sky.

"Look? At what?" He blinked as he lifted his head. All he could see was darkness and ... a single white snowflake floating down. It landed on the tip of his nose, then melted.

"See!" J.D. cried, ecstatic. "I told you! I told you it was waiting to come down at the right time." She let out a whoop as more flakes rained down on them.

He was about to say something to contradict her, but the pure joy on his mate's face made him stop. Instead, he put one arm around his grandmother, and another around his mate, then looked up to the heavens to watch a true Christmas miracle happen.

Epilogue

The snow-covered grounds of Blackstone Castle were the perfect setting for a Christmas wedding, as if it was all laid out and planned, and not even the season and weather could go against the bride's wishes.

"Are you ready—hey, stop peeking!" Damon admonished. "Cam is out there, he'll see you."

J.D. let out an impatient sound and whipped around. "Aww, I just wanted a peek. I didn't have time to look at the setup because Anna Victoria had me up at the crack of dawn to get me ready."

Gabriel pulled her away from the window of the second-floor anteroom right above the patio. "You'll see it in five minutes when you walk down the aisle."

"Aww, this sucks. I can't even watch you all walking out." She put on a pout.

"Yeah, well, you're the bride. Comes with the territory." He dragged her to the sofa. "Now sit and behave."

She crossed her arms over her chest. "Fine."

The wedding coordinator, a bespectacled young man

named Finn peeked his head in. "We're about to start, if you wouldn't mind following me downstairs ..."

"Er, I need a minute!" she cried.

"A minute?" Gabriel said incredulously. "You've done nothing but complain the last couple months that this moment couldn't come soon enough, and *now* you need a minute?"

"It's uh ... a girl thing! Please. I swear, I just have to adjust ... something." She glanced down at her breasts.

Gabriel rolled his eyes. "Fine. Don't be too long, okay?"

Damon sent her a warning look as he walked toward the door with Gabriel. "You behave now, okay?"

"Yes, *mom*," she mocked. "Go. I'll be down in a sec. Finn will make sure I'm there, right?"

"Once you hear the music, start making your way down, and that should leave you plenty of time," Finn said before he and the two other men left the room.

Once they were gone, J.D. shot to her feet. *Finally!* Picking up the skirts of her gown, she rushed back to the window to look out onto the patio again. She was so glad Matthew Lennox had agreed to let them have the wedding and reception here in Blackstone Castle. But then again, as the dragon shifter had said, they were family now.

God, she still couldn't believe that she was getting married. But here they were.

Pushing her nose up to the window, she peered down into the garden. The decor was holiday themed, of course, with red, green, and gold as the main colors, and the castle was bedecked with ribbons, holly, evergreen, and wreaths inside and out. Chairs were laid out in rows on the great stone patio, leaving an aisle in the middle. At the end of the aisle was a raised dais, and instead of a typical arbor, two Christmas trees flanked the black-robed judge waiting for the bride and groom. And of course, the spectacular Blackstone Mountains stood as the perfect backdrop for the scene.

The orchestra began to play Canon in D, and everyone settled in their seats. Cam, looking *abso-fucking-lutely* hot in his formal tux, came out first, followed by his best man, Anders. It was hard to think that a year ago Cam and Anders were the most bitter of enemies due to their opposite natures. But somehow, they met in the middle, shared many patrols together, and were now the best of friends. Cam had said that in their time together, he'd learned that Anders truly was an honorable and admirable man. Though if anyone were to ask the tiger shifter, he would say that it was mostly because Cam had finally gotten that stick out of his ass.

When they finished their walk and stood at the dais, it was time for the three flower girls and ring bearer to make their appearance. The more senior flower girls, Temperance and Her Highness, Princess Natalia of Zaratena, walked hand in hand as they scattered flower petals on the aisle. However, since the last two of their party, Aiden Stevens and Lila Cooper, were still only a few months old and couldn't walk, they were carried in by their mothers.

They were followed by the two bridesmaids, Sarah and Dutchy, who were, coincidentally, both in the advanced stages of pregnancy. Their mates, who partnered them as groomsmen, both walked stiffly beside them, perhaps because the two men were feeling overly protective of their mates and cubs.

Last of course, were the co-maids—er, men of honor. Gabriel had joked to Damon that they should hold hands, an idea which was promptly shut down by the chief. So instead, they walked side by side with the lion shifter preening and raising his hands so as to encourage the crowd to cheer, while his counterpart rolled his eyes.

"Ms. McNamara!" came a frantic voice.

"What? I wasn't doing anything!" J.D. jumped away from the window and whirled around.

Finn stood by the doorway, face red from exertion. "You were supposed to come a while ago—"

"Yeah, yeah!" Rushing over to him, she blew past the poor wedding coordinator and dashed down the grand staircase toward the double glass doors that led to the patio. By the time she got there, the music had already changed—to a classical arrangement of a certain love song that brought a smile to her face each time she heard it.

"Go, go," Finn cried, practically pushing her out.

"All right, all right, hold your godamm—" Her mouth clamped shut as she staggered forward, barely catching herself as she nearly tripped over her skirt.

Since she hadn't worn one in the entire year, J.D. relented and agreed to an actual dress for her wedding. But having no clue about fashion, and having left the design and details to the talented Dutchy Forrester, if anyone asked the bride to describe it, the only thing she could say was it was white and had pockets. Her most treasured accessory, however, was the simple bouquet of roses and ivy she carried, which had a miniature photo of her father and mother tucked in between the flowers. Her arm was also left bare, her tattoo matching the ivy leaves in her bouquet.

As she reached the end of the aisle, she winked at her groom. The look of awe on his face was unmistakable, so just for fun, she stuck out her tongue and crossed her eyes, prompting him to laugh. Judge Cornelius Atherton was not amused as he shot the bride a disapproving look.

The ceremony was quick, simple, and thankfully, uninterrupted. When Atherton pronounced them husband and wife, a cheer erupted from the guests.

"Finally," Cam said as he took her in his arms.

"He hasn't said you may kiss the bride," J.D. pointed out.

Cam turned to the judge. "Sir, if you please?"

The judge smirked. "You may kiss the bride."

"Thanks." And so, he did.

The crowd whooped and cheered for them again, but it was like they were in their own world as they continued to kiss.

"All right, all right, break it up, there are children watching," Gabriel groaned. "Save some for the honeymoon. I'm hungry. And that cake Temperance made looks so good."

"Don't you dare, Russel," J.D. warned as she released Cam's lips. "If I see one bite—"

"C'mon now, love," Cam said. "Let's go."

Everyone was ushered into the castle, toward the ballroom, which was also decorated with the same Christmas holiday theme as the patio. The music played, and the bridal party made their grand entrance, and Cam and J.D. performed their first dance as man and wife to a more traditional waltz.

"Woohoo, didn't know you had it in you, Jasmine Dawn," Anders jeered as they stepped off the dance floor.

J.D. rolled her eyes. After she lost a bet and had to reveal to Anders what her animal was, he was now trying to guess what J.D. stood for. His guesses became more and more ridiculous each time.

"Some village out there is looking for their idiot," J.D. shot back. "I'll make sure to let them know where you are."

"How about Journey Delaware?" the tiger shifter asked. "Jade Destiny?"

"Where do you come up with these?" J.D. rolled her eyes. "They all sound like stripper names."

"Yeah, you would know, Jaylene Danica," Anders snorted. "You're the one who wanted to go to a strip club for your bachelorette party."

"You what?" Cam exclaimed.

"Nothing!" J.D. grabbed her new husband by the arm. "C'mon, let's go sit so they can serve dinner."

They sat at the sweetheart's table in front of the room and everyone soon settled down so they could begin the evening's festivities. As was customary, the toasts began during dinner, and the very first one was given by Her Royal Highness, Princess Natalia.

"Good evening, everyone," the princess began as she stood in front, microphone in hand. "I'd like to make this 'short and sweet' as you Americans say, so don't worry, you don't have to listen to this old woman ramble on." The crowd laughed. "All my life I have been praying for my dear grandson's happiness. I wished for him to find true joy, wherever that may be. Let me tell you, I was just as surprised as you all were when I found out who his mate turned out to be." Chuckles rumbled across the room. "But I have never seen a more perfect couple, who complements each other so well. And in J.D., my dear Aleksandr has continued to discover true happiness, and I wish them well. I love you both." She raised a glass. "And so, please do raise your glasses and give a toast to Their Graces, Cameron Aleksandr Spenser and James Dean McNamara Spenser, the Duke and Duchess of Westmoreland."

"James Dean?" Cam exclaimed. "Your name is *James Dean*?"

J.D. burst out laughing. "Yeah. Pop thought I would be a boy. But Ma loved the name and kept it anyway."

"And you told my grandmother before me? What about the judge? Are we legally married?

"It's all in the paperwork, and I swore him to secrecy," she said. "It's all good, don't worry about it."

Natalia came to them after the toast to hug and kiss them. "Congratulations again. You don't know how happy you both have made me."

"Aww, we love you too, Babs."

Cam rolled his eyes every time she used her nickname for Natalia, but the princess was tickled pink by it. "How are things in the Northern Isles, *Babushka*? And Uncle Sasha?"

"As well as can be." Her eyes sparkled, and she took J.D.'s hands in hers. "This is your doing, *Kotyonok*. If it wasn't for you, we never would have found him."

They were all still shocked at the turn of events earlier in the year when in fact, Natalia's tip did ultimately lead to the lost prince. Of course, it wasn't how anybody thought it would turn out to be, and the road to finding him had been long and arduous. Thank goodness the Dragon Guards were up to the task, though there were many surprises along the way.

Cam groaned. "I can't believe you gave up another favor from a dragon," he said. "You have no idea the things he could do for you. What kinds of rewards he can give you."

J.D. snorted. "What would I have asked for? More money? Another house? Another car? I only have one ass to sit down on."

"And you say I have a way with words."

They finished their dinner, sat through more toasts—and more eye-rolling from Cam as Anders and Gabriel delivered a hilarious joint best man and man of honor speech complete with a slideshow.

The reception continued on with more merriment, eating, drinking, and dancing. J.D. coaxed Cam to play the piano again, though he declined to sing, which was fine with her because she wanted to keep her new husband's voice all to herself anyway.

Surrounded by their family and friends, J.D. couldn't help but feel the love flowing around them. And she couldn't believe this day had finally come. They were now husband and wife. It had taken them this long, not just because she had wanted to be married on Christmas—and thus making sure Cam never had any reason to hate the holiday—but because Cam had to do a lot of traveling back and forth between Colorado and Russia.

As Stepan had promised, the Dashokovs released Natalia from the blood oath. But there was a lot of work to be done to transfer over all the power in the company over to Stepan. Cam still had to sit on the board of directors, but that meant he needed to travel to Russia once a year at most. J.D. had gone with him when he signed the last of the papers, then they helped Natalia pack up her flat in St. Petersburg so she could move to the Northern Isles and they could meet Uncle Sasha. It was there that Cam proposed, and she accepted.

When the party was winding down, Cam whispered in her ear. "Want to go sneak off somewhere with me?"

"Where are we going?"

"Does it matter, as long as we're together?"

She grinned at him. "Lead the way."

Cam led her out of the ballroom, toward the front door of the castle. "I have a surprise for you," he said they walked out.

"A surprise?" she asked. "What—holy moly! Are you shitting me, Spenser?"

He laughed. "No, I'm not. Go ahead." He gestured to the car sitting in the driveway.

"That's a 1958 Rolls-Royce Silver Wraith!" Rushing over to the car, she ran her hands over the smooth body. "Oh, baby. You're a beaut."

"It's yours. Do you like it?"

"Are you fucking kidding me?" she shouted. "Of course I do. I love it!" Launching herself at him, she wrapped her arms around his neck. "I love you, champ."

"And I love you, James Dean." He frowned. "I'm never going to get used to that."

"Why do you think I go by my initials? I was already teased enough as a kid. When we moved here, I decided to just use J.D."

"Well, I love you. Whatever your name is."

As he pressed his mouth to hers, she melted against him. The mate bond flowed between them like a living, breathing thing that bound them in a way that could never be broken. Through the connection, she could feel Cam's love, tenderness, and warmth, and she returned it until the emotions were one and the same.

When they finally pulled apart, her brows knitted together and she pouted.

"What's wrong *now*?" he asked.

"It's really been a great day. But weeeell ... you know what would make *this* the bestest, most perfect Christmas ever?"

"Oh, bloody hell." He shut his eyes tight. "Don't even say it. I swear to God, you're going to shake my faith in science, wife."

"Fine." She snuck a look up at the sky as she spotted a puffy white flake descend from the heavens. "I won't say it." With a soft, satisfied sigh, she pressed her mouth to his.

The End

Dear Reader,

While this may be the end of the Rangers Series, we're not going to leave the world of Blackstone yet!

So many more mysteries to explore in this universe.

Like what happened to a certain dragon guard who visited Blackstone in book 3.

And how did they find the lost Grand Duke?

You'll find out in the next series,

The Dragon Guards of the Northern Isles

Coming 2021.

Sign up for my newsletter now to find out the moment it releases, plus other fun stuff including a chance to win monthly prizes!

Turn the page for authors notes!

All the best,

Alicia

Author's Notes
WRITTEN NOVEMBER 25, 2020

It's been a while since I've written any authors notes - I'm not really sure anyone's reading them and after a while, I've run out of things to say, especially when a book leaves me so emotionally drained (in a satisfying way).

But considering what a year we've all had and this being the final book not only in the Blackstone Rangers series, but also the final book I've written in 2020, I thought it was only apt to write these notes. I've gone over past notes from a few years back and realize how much I enjoyed writing them, taking you along through the process of my writing, and giving you little tidbits and trivia along the way.

I'm sure like me, many of you started out this year with much anticipation. The New Year always gives us all a chance to start fresh. Little did we know what a tumultuous year it would be.

At the end of 2019 I planned out my entire year - finish the last three books in the True Mates Generations series, perform in at least two theater productions, and then go on an extended vacation in the summer. Then perhaps I would start a brand new series in the fall, something in the Blackstone universe, which I've missed so much.

However, when March 2020 rolled around and the world shut down (because of the dreaded V word), I had to put those plans aside. There was no travel and no live performances anywhere. Well, I managed to finish True Mates, and since I had to cancel all performing and vacation plans, I dove right into Blackstone Rangers.

The Rangers weren't my next planned series when I wrote the original Blackstone Mountain books. If you recall, I focused a lot on Deputy Cole Carson and Fire Chief Will Mason. I really really wanted to do Police or Fire next (though I did set up the Rangers in Blackstone Wolf, but we don't even meet Damon then). Or I was going to do a dragon series, featuring the Dragon Guards or the Silver or Air Dragons.

However, I really wanted to tell Dutchy's story, and Dutchy really *really* wanted Krieger as a mate. You should read about the conversations I have with my characters, which I send out to subscribers of my newsletter.

I tried, I REALLY tried to convince her to find another mate, but she wouldn't have it! And her and Krieger's story has been in my head for so long, I really needed it out. And so I decided, with lockdowns in place and plenty of time in my hands, I could finish the Blackstone Rangers Series this year.

But wait!

There's more!

Blackstone Rangers was going to end with Dutchy and Krieger. That scene of them looking up at the stars at the end was how I wanted it to end. It was so clear in my mind. The perfect ending.

But then J.D. climbed out of my computer and and threatened to kill me if I didn't give her a Happy Ever After.

And since she pretty much barreled her way into the rangers' lives, she wanted to be part of this series too, despite not being a ranger herself. I protested, but she had a few choice words for me!

(Again, I send these conversations out occasionally on my newsletter. Make sure you subscribe!)

Oh and if THAT wasn't complicated enough, it HAD to be a Christmas book.

(Because J.D. loves Christmas, y'all).

And so that's how this book came about. Cameron Spenser was going to be a nerdy librarian wolf shifter, but polar bears are the perfect shifter animal for Christmas, right? (Hello, they're Santa's neighbor in the North Pole!)

Cam was the perfect mate for J.D. His coldness is really a mask for his awkwardness, which I thought was so adorable and very different from the usual alpha-hole characters we read about.

Plus, neither of them wanted to fight their fate, which I thought was refreshing. However, I had to somehow throw a few obstacles in their way, because otherwise it would be a very short (and boring) story. And as we all know, love isn't always easy and if we want something, we have to fight for it.

I really hope you enjoy this story. It's a labor of love for you, my dear reader. It's because of you I get to do this thing I love and I wake up every day thankful for this chance to tell you these stories.

And, I think after the year we've ALL had, we deserve some lighthearted fun, heartwarming romance, and a little Christmas magic.

With much love,

Alicia